Heir of Deception

by
Joanne Liggan

Llumina Press

Copyright 2002 Joanne Liggan

All rights reserved. No part of this publication may be reproduced or transmitted in any form or by any means electronic or mechanical, including photocopy, recording, or any information storage and retrieval system, without permission in writing from both the copyright owner and the publisher.

Requests for permission to make copies of any part of this work should be mailed to Permissions Department, Llumina Press, P.O. Box 772246, Coral Springs, Florida 33077-2246.

ISBN: 1-932047-69-7

Printed in the United States of America.

DEDICATION

I dedicate this novel to my dear friend, Aimée West, who encouraged me and helped with the finishing touches and editing. You have been a bright star in my life and I praise God for your friendship.

Joanne

To Leona,
I hope you enjoy Rachel's story.
May God bless you and yours.

Love,
Joanne Liggan

10-8-05

PROLOGUE

Midnight, Saturday, June 2, in Eastridge

Coughing, choking, gasping for breath. Drowning. Rachel fought the suffocating pain on her chest and heard screams in the distance. Then she awoke, but the nightmare remained. Breathing was difficult. Acrid smoke engulfed her nose and throat as she groped for the switch on the lamp beside the bed and clicked it on. The haze was so dense she could see only a few feet in front of her. Seconds later, the light flickered and everything went dark. Screams came from down the hall—'*Lucille!*' Rachel scrambled from the covers and ran toward her closed door. Heat penetrated through the wood panels. '*It's so hot—opening it might be fatal.*' She stood there coughing, trying to decide what to do. She could no longer breathe. She dropped to the floor and crawled across the room to the outside balcony doors. Dizziness overcame her. She struggled to reach up for the doorknob, pushing the doors open and gasping for air. She scrambled out and slammed the doors closed behind her to keep from feeding the fire more oxygen. It took a moment for the fresh air to fill her lungs and revive her enough to stand. She ran to Collin's door and, finding it locked, pounded on it, wailing at him to wake up. When there was no response, she leaned over the balcony railing and shouted for help. The fire roared so loud she could no longer hear the screaming from the other room.

A hand grabbed her from behind and wrapped a wet blanket around her, covering her face. Then a frantic male voice told her to take a deep breath and hang on. She was swept from her feet, the deafening roar of the flames and the intense heat infiltrating the soggy wool as he carried her through the house, down the blazing hallway and descended the stairs. Just as he placed her on the ground a good distance from the inferno, fire engines and rescue squads arrived. Her rescuer disappeared back into the fiery hell as an EMS paramedic checked her over for burns and gave her oxygen.

Everything was reeling. She was inside an ambulance rushing to the hospital. She recalled the screaming, "Did everyone get out okay?" Her voice was weak.

The paramedic was attempting to place the oxygen mask over her mouth and nose. "I don't know, but I promise I'll let you know something as soon as I hear."

At the hospital, she was checked over thoroughly once again and placed in a large room with several beds separated by curtains. Left alone for what seemed like hours, she was about to doze off when someone touched her hand. Her eyes opened to Nathan, covered in soot, gazing down at her, looking worried.

She was so weak and tired, having difficulty just keeping her eyes open, but she needed answers. "What..."

"Shhhh. Don't try to talk. They gave you a sedative so you'll rest. You inhaled a lot of smoke, but you'll be fine. Just rest. I'll stay here until you wake up, and then we'll talk." Nathan patted her hand to reassure her.

Although anxious to know what happened and if everyone else was all right, the medication prevailed, and she drifted off to sleep.

CHAPTER 1

Two months earlier, Friday, April 13, in Wapiti

Oblivious to the weather and the fact that all the townspeople had long since left the small cemetery, lost in the intense pain that gripped her soul, Rachel Brittain stared at the freshly covered grave. Rain trickled over her face, merging with the tears that spilled from dark eyes. Heavy rain-glistened black hair lay on her neck and shoulders.

Rachel had been at her mother's side through those last awful days, caring for her, praying for her and willing her to get well, only to watch her slip away. She had escorted the pallbearers to the gravesite; hand on the casket, not wanting to let go. To turn and walk across the road to the little dwelling that she and her mother had called home was to surrender to the ache deep within and admit that she was, at only twenty years old, alone.

Goosebumps rose on her bronze flesh as she folded her arms against the chill. A threadbare cotton dress clung to her tall slender frame.

She gazed into the distance. A few hundred feet in front of her was a cliff that overlooked green valleys and foothills. Taking a deep breath and gathering her strength, she turned and began the short journey across the field to the empty house, examining the weather-beaten cottage her mother had tried so desperately to make a good home. Faded green paint, crooked shutters, and a tattered roof, yet the little home had kept out the rain and kept Rachel warm and secure in her mother's love.

She approached the lane that separated her property from the cemetery and noticed an elderly man trudging up the road with his body bent against the blowing rain. When he saw Rachel, a slight smile emerged through his white whiskers. "My car broke down a mile or so up the road. Could you maybe tell me where I might find a service station?" There was gentleness in his faded eyes.

"There's a station about a half mile further down the road."

"Much obliged." Touching the brim of his brown tweed fedora, he continued past her.

"Wait! You're gonna catch your death of cold if you keep going in this rain. Why don't you come on inside and dry off. I'll fix us a pot of coffee while you wait for the rain to stop."

Gratitude flowed from his gray eyes as he nodded in agreement.

They drenched a few towels and became reasonably dry. Rachel quietly poured two cups of coffee, placing them with the sugar and cream on the small kitchen table, and then stirred the fire in the cast-iron, potbellied wood stove. Finally, she sat across the table from where her visitor had already claimed a seat.

He wrapped his hands around the steaming cup and took a sip. "This coffee sure hits the spot. It's just what I needed. Looks like I'm not the only one that got caught out in the rain. What were you doin' walking around out there?"

Rachel stared into her cup. "I was coming from the cemetery. We just buried my mother. I had a hard time making myself come back home to face the loneliness."

His expression softened, his eyes sincere as he spoke. "I'm truly sorry about your mother. You want to talk about her?"

She did feel the need to talk. She didn't know why, but she wanted this stranger to know what a wonderful person her mother had been. "Momma struggled hard to raise me all alone. We never had too much, but we managed okay. We kept our little garden going so we had plenty to eat. We would freeze or can some food to carry us through the winter months. Momma worked different kinds of jobs that came up around town. She cleaned for people and kept the store some. And whenever Doc wasn't around or was too busy, she would help with the sick or mid-wife. Everyone knew they could call on Jessie Brittain whenever they needed help. The townsfolk have been real nice to me since Momma got sick. They would bring baskets of food over or help me tend to her. I knew she was dying, but..." She choked as she tried to hold back the tears burning her eyes.

The old man listened quietly. "She sounds like a mighty fine woman." He turned and gazed thoughtfully out of the window. "Well, looks as if the rain has stopped. The sun is peeking through the clouds. Everything is always more beautiful after a good rain, don't you think?" He gathered his trench coat and hat and walked outside. "Thank you for your hospitality. It was kind of you to bother with me at such a difficult time."

"I had selfish reasons for inviting you in. By your being here, the house isn't so empty."

"And here I thought you were just a generous person." He winked at her and then looked to the sky. "They say in every cloud is a silver lining. I don't really know about silver linings, but I do know that everything seems a lot more clear and bright after a storm—like a renewal or cleansing, as if the rain has cleansed the earth's soul. You know, life is just like that. Once you get past the stormy parts, things brighten up." He took a few steps toward the road, then turned back to look at her, cocking his head. "You got any other family around? Aunts or Uncles?" He seemed genuinely concerned.

"No. Momma was an only child."

"What about your father?"

"I never knew my father." *Because the son-of-a-bitch never married Momma.*

CHAPTER 2

Monday, April 16, still in Wapiti

Rachel prepared for the spring, planning the kinds of vegetables she would plant in the small garden and the types of flowers she would grow in the flowerbeds. She walked around the yard surveying what had to be done and thought about the visitor she'd encountered the day of the funeral and his remarks concerning the storm. Her mother had loved the rain and often remarked how it renewed the earth's beauty and washed away the impurities. Rachel believed with all her heart that her mother had sent this man to comfort her.

She went inside and retrieved an old rusty cookie tin from the kitchen drawer. Inside was the meager amount of cash left of her mother's savings. After counting it, she realized she couldn't afford flower seeds. She'd have to make every penny count toward food. The garden would probably be all she could handle by herself, and she wasn't even sure she could manage that.

The walk to Mr. Warren's store was refreshing with the bright sunshine and a warm southern breeze thawing the chill from the night before. The store was the only one in the small Appalachian town of Wapiti and served as the grocery, pharmacy, feed and seed, hardware supply and post office. As she entered the cluttered store, the screen door creaked and slammed shut behind her. Familiar smells of smoked meats and fresh baked bread greeted her. Her shoes announced her arrival on the scarred pine plank floor.

Ed Warren peeked over the meat counter. "Good morning, Rachel. What can I do for you today?"

"Hi Mr. Warren. I just need to pick up a few groceries and get some things to start my garden. I hope I'm not too late getting things planted. I believe we usually have things in the ground by now."

"Oh, I think you'll be okay if you plant soon. It's not too terribly late yet. Go ahead and help yourself. Just holler if you need help finding anything."

She wandered through the store, choosing the items she needed, then stopped at a magazine stand to flip through the pages of a *Better Homes and Gardens* publication. Pictures of beautiful houses and flower gardens stared back at her. Rachel had spent hours looking through such magazines and dreaming about what life must be like in other parts of the world. *No sense wasting time on pipe dreams. I guess I'll be stuck in this town forever.*

Mr. Warren was adding up her purchases when they both heard the sputter of an engine and looked out the window at a shiny dark blue, very expensive-looking car parked in front of the store. Craning his neck and squinting to see, Mr. Warren observed, "Now I wonder who that is showing up here in a Mercedes?"

Rachel continued to watch, trying to see the car's occupant. No one in Wapiti had a vehicle to compare to this one. A stout, very well dressed woman with short bleached hair slowly emerged from the driver's seat. *Definitely out of place in this rough country.*

Mr. Warren smiled from ear to ear. "Well I'll be damned....if it ain't Lucille Chavis!" He rushed to the door and welcomed the woman into the store. "Well Lucille, what the hell are you doin' up around these parts?"

"Hello Ed. How is everyone around here doing?"

"Oh, same as always, 'cept for the loss of Jessie, of course. We're all gonna miss her somethin' awful."

"Yes, I know. That's why I've come." She glanced at Rachel who had been standing back watching the reunion of old friends.

"Hello," Rachel smiled, wondering what this woman had to do with her mother.

"Hello, Rae, I'm Lucille Chavis." She offered her hand in greeting.

Rachel stood motionless, her heart quickening at the sound of the familiar nickname and surprise showing on her face.

"I'm sorry, I didn't mean to startle you. Did your mother tell you about me?"

Still speechless, Rachel shook her head.

Mr. Warren came to her rescue. "Lucille, I believe Rachel is just surprised to hear someone call her Rae. It was a pet name that Jessie used for her a lot."

"Oh--, well that's how your mother always referred to you when I talked to her, so I just assumed that's what everyone called you..." her voice faded. "I'm so sorry about your mother. I came as soon as I heard about her passing. I hope she didn't suffer."

"No, she went quietly in her sleep."

Lucille fidgeted with her pearl necklace, obviously unsure of what to say next. Rachel began gathering her purchases. "So you knew Momma?"

"Oh yes. She was a friend of mine when you were just a toddler. We didn't see each other much, but we kept in touch with letters. You've never heard her mention the name Chavis?"

Again Rachel shook her head.

Looking puzzled, Lucille continued. "I don't know why she wouldn't have told you about me. But I told her that she needn't worry about you if anything was to ever happen to her. She used to worry a lot about what would happen to you if she weren't around to take care of you. She seemed to be relieved after I told her that you would always be welcome in our home."

"That was very kind of you, but..."

"Oh, I wasn't just being kind. I meant it. And now I want you to know that the offer still stands. You deserve to have a good, full life."

Rachel was becoming very uncomfortable with what this woman was suggesting. "Mr. Warren, how much do I owe you?"

Mr. Warren, who had been quietly listening to their conversation, waved her away. "Oh, don't worry about that now. I'll just put it on your tab. You can pay me later."

"Are you sure?"

"Of course. I know where you live." His eyes sparkled as he grinned.

Rachel smiled back at him and headed for the door carrying her two grocery bags. "Nice to meet you Mrs. Chavis."

Lucille looked at Mr. Warren and then back at Rachel. "Rachel, could I please give you a lift back to your house? I'd really like to talk to you some more."

Rachel stopped as she reached the door, then turned and looked Lucille squarely in the eye. "I don't mean to be rude, but I really had rather walk, thank you."

Lucille looked at Mr. Warren, beckoning for his help. He walked over to the door to hold it open for Rachel. "Enjoy your walk home. I'll bring Lucille over to see you later on, after she and I have had a chance to visit."

Rachel knew that Mr. Warren would look out for her. He always had. "Thank you."

It was a beautiful April afternoon. She watched the birds gathering twigs and other nest-building materials as she prepared the ground for planting. The old rough-handled hoe she retrieved from the shed was rusty and dull, but the ground was still soft from the rain and was easily tilled. She removed the grass and weeds from the turned soil and punched holes for the seeds. Then she heard the purr of an engine and looked up to see the dark blue car stop in front of her home. It had only been a few hours since she had seen them at the store. Rachel sighed and spoke softly to herself, "I'm really not up for this right now."

Mr. Warren and Mrs. Chavis waved as they climbed from the vehicle.

Trying to smile and be the gracious hostess her mother had taught her to be, Rachel invited them in to sit at the kitchen table while she washed her hands. Wiping her hands on a ragged towel, she finally joined them. Mr. Warren took charge of the conversation as he addressed Rachel. "Lucille and her husband, Raymond, used to live here some years back. When they heard about your mother's passing, they were worried about you, so Lucille just came up here to make sure you were all right."

"Well, as you can see, I'm fine. But I appreciate your concern."

Mr. Warren continued. "It's really more than just concern. They told your mother that they would watch over you if anything ever happened to her."

Mrs. Chavis quickly added, "She seemed to be comforted by the fact that someone would be here for you. She worried about what would happen to you." She looked at Ed Warren, beckoning him on.

He looked at the older woman as if he were having a difficult time deciding what to say next. "What we are trying to tell you, Rachel, is that Mr. and Mrs. Chavis would like for you to come stay with them for a while in their home."

Rachel shook her head. "That's very sweet of you, but I can't possibly leave here. This is my home. A home Momma worked hard to keep for me and where I was raised. I need to stay here and take care of the garden."

Lucille reached across the table and laid her hand over Rachel's. "I understand that dear. We're just talking about a short visit for right now. I'll bring you right back home whenever you're ready."

"But, like I said, I can't leave the garden right now."

Mr. Warren had been a close and dear friend for many years. Rachel trusted him and watched him closely as he stood and walked to the sink, retrieved a glass from the cupboard and filled it with tap water. "Don't worry about the garden. I'll be glad to take care of it while you're gone. You can get it planted, and I'll make sure it gets plenty of water. There's not that much else to do until the plants begin coming in."

Rachel looked at him. "You sound like you think I should go?"

"Well, I think it might be a good idea. You'll get to see a whole other way of life. Stuck up here in these hills is no life for a young girl like yourself. You should experience more of what life has to offer. Raymond and Lucille live in Eastridge. It's not a huge city, but it has a lot more to offer than this place. It's just down in the foothills, not so far away. So, if you don't like it, you can always come home."

Rachel's mouth was suddenly very dry. She stood and walked to the sink to get herself a glass of water. Staring into the sink with her back to her guests, she shook her head. "No, I don't think so. I think I should stay right here."

Mr. Warren walked up behind her and placed his hand on her shoulder. "Honey, you just think about it for awhile. Lucille is gonna stay in town tonight, and you can discuss the idea more tomorrow after you've had a chance to sleep on it. Come on, Lucille, let's go get you settled in for the night."

Rachel turned to see desperation in Lucille's eyes as she looked at Mr. Warren and then at her. "Please consider it, Rachel. I will be greatly disappointed if you won't come home with me. Raymond and I were so looking forward to you visiting us. And I honestly believe that's what Jessie would have wanted for you."

After they left, Rachel paced around the kitchen trying to sort out what had happened. *This stranger shows up out of nowhere and Ed Warren, whose opinion I truly respect, actually believes I should leave town with this person. Is this really what Momma would have wanted?*

Though exhausted from the day's planting, she tossed and turned all night trying to decide what to do. She considered her life as it was in this dying settlement where there were very few people her age. Most of her schoolmates had moved away to find a better life. She wondered what it was like beyond the mountains and valleys she knew so well. *It would be interesting to see another part of the world. But I don't know this woman and her husband. But Mr. Warren obviously thought it would be all right. Maybe a short visit wouldn't hurt.* It was almost dawn when she finally drifted off to sleep.

The loneliness hung heavy in the air around her as she walked into the cool kitchen and prepared breakfast. Although not at all hungry, this had been her morning ritual for as long as she could remember. She removed the eggs from the refrigerator and stood looking at them, realizing she didn't need but one from now on. Her mother was gone. She wouldn't be eating with her anymore. Tears streamed down her cheeks. Her heart ached. She sat at the table and looked around the quiet lifeless room. Her mother had always been singing or humming in the mornings. Of course, that was before she got sick. Even then, Rachel had been so intent on caring for her that she hadn't noticed how quiet the mornings had been. But now.....

She walked around the lonely house, room by room. The void within her chest felt heavier when she saw her mother's empty bed. Rachel's entire life, since her early teens, had been spent taking care of her mother. That was all she had known. *I wonder what kind of life I could have someplace else, in another town where there are opportunities and people my own age.* Her heart began to pound with excitement at the thought of what could be awaiting her.

Suddenly there didn't seem to be any reason to stay.

Later that morning, they were once again seated around the kitchen table, Lucille fidgeting with her pearl necklace, and Ed Warren quietly watching and waiting, giving Rachel one of his warm, comforting smiles. He had always been a calming influence in her life, probably the closest thing she would get to a father figure or grandfather. Rachel looked at both of them and took a deep breath. "Okay, I'll go."

The older woman's face glowed with satisfaction. "Wonderful!"

"But just for a visit. I just need to get away from here for a little while. Just so I don't feel so alone."

Trying not to push too hard, Lucille unsuccessfully attempted to stifle her enthusiasm. "How long do you need to get packed?"

"It won't take long. I'll just throw together a few clothes."

She placed several pair of old jeans and some shirts into a grocery bag and folded her only cotton dress.

Lucille sat on Rachel's bed and watched, noticed the limited wardrobe, and shook her head. "We're going to have to go shopping for some clothes first thing. How are you going to catch yourself a man with these?"

Men didn't interest Rachel in the least. She didn't trust them, not only because of what her father had done, but also because of the numerous other men who had been a part of her mother's life. They had taken advantage of her mother's kind heart to manipulate her into many heartbreaks. Never becoming a cold person, forgiving each man that hurt her and blaming herself for all her troubles, she always begged Rachel not to grow hard-hearted, but told her to be more careful of her choices than she had been. From where Rachel watched, it had looked as if all men were the same, and none of them were worth crying over. Now that she was twenty, she felt the desires a woman naturally feels, but was determined she would allow no man to use or hurt her in any way.

Keeping her thoughts quietly to herself, she collected a few personal items and placed them in another paper bag. She glanced at Lucille, but the other woman was too busy collecting the bags into her arms to notice the coldness in Rachel's eyes or the determined set of her jaw.

They wound their way down the mountain, Rachel feeling completely drained from the rapid change in her normally quiet life. Lucille glanced at her and smiled warmly. "Dear, you look tired. Why don't you put your head back and take a nap. It's going to be a while before we get to a town with a decent restaurant. So go on to sleep. I'll wake you when I find a place."

"But I don't have enough money with me to be going to a restaurant."

"Oh, it's my treat. Don't concern yourself with that."

"Well, I am hungry, and I promise I'll pay you back."

Rachel's stomach fluttered with nervousness, and her mind raced with a million questions. She had no intention of falling asleep even though she had slept very little in the last two days. She wanted to see everything and enjoy the ride. She laid her head back on the headrest and closed her eyes to sort out her thoughts.

Before leaving home, she had walked across the road and visited her mother's grave where she found a beautiful arrangement of fresh flowers. *I wonder who could have put those there.*

The car came to a halt. She opened her eyes to a neon sign that read *Larson's Café.*

"Well, hello. Did you sleep well?"

"Are we out of the mountains already?" Her voice was still sleepy as she sat up in the seat, yawning.

"Oh, yes. We've been out of the hills for about fifteen minutes. I've heard that the food at this place is pretty good. Shall we give it a try?"

Rachel straightened her clothes and her hair and followed her companion into the pretty colonial building. There was a small lobby with dark red crushed velvet chairs and sofa and glass tables with brass trim. To the left was a line of hungry people waiting to get their trays.

After a few minutes, they finally came to the serving area. Rachel had never seen so much good food at one time in her life! There was such a variety of choices in meats and vegetables. And then there were all kinds of bread and tasty desserts!

When they sat at a small corner table, Lucille seemed to be enjoying a private joke. "Rae, your eyes almost popped right out of your head when you saw all that food." She laughed.

Rachel smiled, imagining how she must have looked. "I hope I didn't embarrass you. It's just that I've never seen so much delicious looking food!"

"No, of course you didn't embarrass me. Enjoy your meal."

And she did.

So many questions still remained unanswered, she wasn't quite sure where to start.

"Mrs. Chavis?"

"Please, Dear, call me Lucille."

"Okay. How did you meet Momma?"

"I was visiting my husband's parents there in your small town." She spoke slowly, obviously choosing her words carefully. "I went for a walk one day and saw your mother playing in the yard with you. You were only eighteen months old and toddling around pretty good. You were headed toward the road, and she was running after you. I watched as she caught you, and both of you giggled as she whirled you playfully around. The laughter was so contagious, I found myself standing in the road laughing along with you. Your mother and I talked for a while and soon became good friends. There weren't very many women around town that were as young as Jessie, so she enjoyed having someone to talk to. She worried a lot about how she would bring you up by herself. She wanted to get married but could never find the right man. I wanted to help her, but there wasn't much I could do except be her friend and let her know I would be there if she ever needed me."

"So your husband came from Wapiti? I don't seem to remember the name Chavis." She tried to think back.

"No, you wouldn't. His parents moved away while you were still a toddler. They came to live with us in Eastridge for a while until they both passed away."

Leaving the restaurant, Rachel felt more relaxed. Knowing Lucille had been a friend to her mother kindled a fondness within Rachel.

The name of the city, Eastridge, was familiar, but she couldn't place where she'd heard it before. She pondered for a few minutes until she finally remembered. "I remember Momma getting a letter from Eastridge when I was younger. It must have been from you."

"Yes, it probably was."

"But it really upset her when she read it. What would you have written to upset her so much?"

"Well, how long ago was it?" Lucille looked puzzled.

"I guess it was about six or seven years ago."

Lucille thought for a minute, then relaxed. "That must have been when I wrote to tell her of the death of my in-laws. She had known them when she was growing up, and it probably disturbed her."

"Yes, maybe that was it." But Rachel still felt unsure. Jessie believed that death was just a door to another world, and everyone would be reunited in that other world one day. The letter had upset her far more than anybody's death would have.

Lucille, noticing Rachel's hesitation, tried again. "Or, it might have been the time we were both counting on my coming to live there. When my husband said he was planning to move up there to live, Jessie and I became so excited about being neighbors that when it fell through, I'm afraid we both reacted like children having their favorite toy taken from us. We both cried about it for weeks."

"If your husband came from Wapiti, then he must have grown up with Momma?"

"I suppose. Raymond doesn't talk about his childhood very much. I gather he had a pretty unhappy time of it when he was a boy. His parents were rather hard on him, so he left home while he was still just a kid."

"And he still took them in when they got old?"

"Sure. They were his parents, and he loved them. People change a lot as they grow older. They can see things more clearly as they learn more about life, and they can understand other people better."

An hour after leaving the restaurant, Lucille turned onto another road. A few miles down that road she announced, "Welcome to Eastridge. I hope you'll like it here."

Rachel watched wide-eyed as they passed the shops, a theater and several other buildings. Another turn and they were driving up a blacktopped circular drive to the Chavis home. It shone a brilliant alabaster in the soft glow of the sunset reminding Rachel of pictures she had seen of old southern plantations, except on a smaller scale. A two-story veranda ran along the entire front and one side of the house. Large columns added the colonial touch.

"It's like looking into a picture book!" Her eyes sparkled with excitement.

"We just had it painted and remodeled last summer, but you should have seen what a terrible sight it was before then." Lucille chuckled while leading her guest into the front door. In front of them, a flight of curved stairs wound to a balcony that overlooked the foyer. Lucille took Rachel's coat and hung it, along with her own, on a wooden coat rack that stood in the corner by the door.

"Raymond?" She waited for a reply.

"I'm in the study." It was a deep, but pleasant voice coming from a distant room.

Lucille took Rachel's hand and led her through a door on their left, through a family room, and into the study.

"Our guest is here. Raymond, this is Rachel Brittain." Lucille looked very pleased with herself as she introduced them. Her husband stood, smiled warmly, and held out his hand. Rachel lightly took his hand, quickly averted her eyes from his, and ended the handshake as soon as possible. She turned to Lucille. "Could you show me the room I will be using so I can freshen up?" Then she realized her rudeness and added apologetically, "I'm a bit weary from the ride."

"Of course. I'll find Collin and have him bring your things in from the car. Come along." They retraced their steps through the family room and into the foyer. Lucille led the way up the stairway to a balcony. There appeared to be two bedrooms on the right side of the house and two on the left with a bath in the middle. Lucille showed her into the room nearest the bathroom. "This will be your room. If you would like to change any of the decor, feel free to do so. It's your room to do with whatever you please."

"Thank you, but it's so beautiful the way it is."

Lucille left her admiring the room, and she could hear the woman's voice echoing through the house as she shouted for Collin. *Who is Collin anyway?* She wanted to ask, but decided it really wasn't important right now. *I'm sure I'll find out soon enough anyway.*

After finding her son and asking him to retrieve Rachel's bags from the car and take them up to her, Lucille went back into the study and found Raymond gazing out of the window, lost in thought. She recognized the vacant look he always got when he was upset about something. He had never been one to show anger, he just withdrew. "Okay, what is it? What's bothering you?"

"You have to ask? Lucy, you shouldn't have brought her here."

"Raymond, we talked about this before I went. I told you I was going to bring her home with me. Can't you just accept it and try to enjoy it?"

"Yes, we talked about it, but you just won't listen to reason. Lucille, I'm telling you, this is a bad idea. I don't understand you. Why would you want to do this?"

"Why can't you understand? I had to. It's the least I could do to try to fix things." She shook her head and threw up her hands. "Well, she's here now, and you're just going to have to deal with it." She stomped out of the room and into the kitchen to start dinner.

Feeling strangely out of kilter, Rachel sat on the bed scrutinizing the room. The walls were covered with soft mint-green wallpaper, which matched perfectly with the carpet. The bedspread and drapes were white, speckled with tiny red roses, giving the room a romantic atmosphere. French doors led to the upper floor of the veranda on the side of the house. She walked out to explore the view and breathed in the pleasing scent of freshly mowed grass. The sun had set, and a purple haze covered the flat horizon. *What am I doing here?* She felt scared, yet excited. Homesick, yet glad to be away. Nervous, yet somehow calmed. She was lost in her own quiet thoughts until a voice behind her broke the silence.

"Beautiful, isn't it."

"Yes it is." She turned to see an extremely confident, and sinfully attractive, man in his early twenties standing in the doorway gazing in the direction she'd been looking. Her pulse quickened. *So this must be Collin.* "I was just thinking how different it looks compared to the mountains back home."

"Homesick, already?" he taunted her.

Insulted by his tone, she threw her hair back and remarked defensively, "Not really. I was just making a comparison."

With a half grin, silently mocking her, he pretended to become businesslike, "Your 'bags' are on your bed, madam. There's no need for a tip. And just yell if you need anything more." He winked as he touched his forehead in a playful salute and disappeared from the room.

CHAPTER 3

Thursday, April 19 in Eastridge

Rachel tried to fit another package into the back seat of the already overflowing Mercedes. "I think I'll just have to hold this one in my lap." She was still leaning into the car and glanced up to see Lucille trying to wedge another package in on the other side of the seat. They both burst into laughter.

"I guess it's time for us to quit." Lucille slammed the door on her side and walked around to hand Rachel the other package. "You can hold this one too."

They had visited nearly every dress shop in the city, plus several sportswear stores and shoe stores. Never having been to a clothing store before now, this had been an entirely new and exhilarating experience for Rachel. In Wapiti, anything that wasn't carried by Mr. Warren's store had to be purchased from catalogs.

On their way home, Lucille stopped the car in front of a hairdressing salon. "Welcome to my little home-away-from-home." She looked proud as she pointed to the sign that read *Lucille's Cut & Curl*. "I just need to check in to make sure everything is okay here."

As soon as they walked through the door, the horrible smell of ammonia and other putrid odors assaulted Rachel's nose. *How could anyone stand to work in here? It really stinks!* She waited in a small sitting area while Lucille disappeared into another room. A minute or two later she returned, "Everything appears to be under control here, so let's go unload our goodies."

They arrived home and were unloading the car when Lucille referred back to their visit to the salon. "Do you think you would be interested in helping out in the salon while you're here?"

"I'm afraid I don't know much about styling hair." *Besides, I couldn't stand that smell!*

"I thought, if you're interested, you could help by doing small jobs like washing hair and booking appointments, and in the meantime you could be watching the other stylists. A sort of on-the-job training. Then later, if you like it and decide to stick around, you could go to school to take a course in cosmetology."

"It sounds like a good idea, but…"

"Good, then it's settled. Tomorrow is Friday. We'll get the paperwork done and get you started."

During the conversation, they succeeded in carrying all the packages to Rachel's room and now had them stacked on the bed. Never stopping to take a breath, Lucille turned to leave the room. "I'll leave you so you can try on your new clothes and get them put away. I've got to get dinner started." And, like a whirlwind, she was gone, leaving Rachel with a mess and feeling bewildered.

Rachel plopped down onto the corner of the bed, causing packages to slide around, falling on her and to the floor. *Why have I allowed this stranger to barge into my life and manipulate me! First she talks me into leaving Wapiti. She made coming here sound so logical. Then there was this shopping trip, which I have to admit was the most fun I've ever had in my whole life. But now, she's deciding my entire career for me. I don't know what kind of job I want, but I don't have the least bit of interest in hair. I've always kept my hair long and straight because it's so easy to just tie it back. And that awful smell!*

She began opening her packages and admiring the new clothes. Her anger at Lucille began to diminish. Now she was feeling obligated to her. *It was so sweet of her to buy me these clothes. I know she means well, but I've just got to think of something I'd rather do to earn my keep around here, if I decide to stay.* However, when she heard Lucille call everyone to dinner, she still had no ideas. There was no choice but to go along with things, at least until she could decide on something better. She'd let herself fall into a very unsavory trap.

The whirlwind continued, with Lucille guiding her around town, dragging her to a school thirty miles outside of Eastridge, checking into the class schedules and gathering brochures, attempting to get her excited about enrolling. Then off to the salon to fill out the paperwork involved with her employment.

Once again, the chemical odors made Rachel's stomach turn as she walked through the waiting room doorway and into the large styling room. First there was the shampoo area and then four stylist stations. A young dark-haired girl was busy wrapping foil around sections of her customer's hair. She glanced up as Lucille and Rachel walked past.

At the back of the building were Lucille's office, the restroom, and a small room with a table, microwave, snack machine, and little refrigerator. Other than the piles of hair on the floor, everything looked immaculate and organized.

"I'll pay you on an hourly basis at minimum wage to start. You won't have any set hours, but can just come in and help out whenever we need you. Most of my time is spent here during the weekdays. On Saturdays I just check in to be sure everything is okay. So a lot of the time that you're here, I might not be, so I want you to meet my right hand girl." She walked out of her office and glanced around. "Milly, what time is Beth due in?"

"She'll be coming in late today. She said she should be here by five."

Lucille returned to her office and began straightening papers that littered her desk. "You'll have to wait to meet Beth tomorrow. Although Milly is a terrific stylist, Beth has the ambition to be a better manager. So I entrust the running of things to her whenever I'm not here. She unlocks in the mornings and locks up at night. She arranges the schedules for the other girls and generally keeps things going. She's young, but very motivated. I think you'll find her a pleasure to work with."

On Saturday morning, Lucille and Rachel returned to the salon, and Rachel was introduced to Beth Sharpe. A pretty blond girl with big blue eyes and clear creamy skin, Beth's hair was tied up with a blue ribbon with soft curls cascading down the back of her head. A couple of small curls framed her face, adding to its perfection. She held her head high, and it seemed to Rachel that her nose was tilted a little too far upward.

Rachel smiled as they were introduced. *She's so flawless she hardly seems real. She looks like a spoiled child trying hard to be a sophisticated woman.*

After returning Rachel to the house, Lucille went back to the salon to help with their hectic Saturday afternoon schedule. They had over-booked appointments and had too much work for the two stylists on duty to handle. It had been decided that Rachel should begin work on Monday when everything was slack so there would be time for her to be instructed more thoroughly. Rachel felt a sense of relief. Lucille was finally leaving her alone. Now maybe she would have a chance to catch her breath.

For the past few days she'd avoided Mr. Chavis and Collin as much as possible. It hadn't been difficult since Lucille had monopolized her time, but there had still been dinners to sit through. She was beginning to feel more comfortable around the older man. He would talk to her about what she and Lucille had done each day. Sometimes she felt he was a bit uncomfortable about her living with them, but thought maybe it was her imagination. And then there was Collin, who always made her uneasy. Although he didn't talk to her much, he always seemed to be watching her and laughing at her.

Rae wandered into the study to find a book to read and found Mr. Chavis in his recliner reading. He glanced up at her, placed a postcard in the book to mark his place and put the book on a table by his chair. To avoid eye contact, she looked down at his book. *Hondo* by Louis L'Amour.

"So, Rachel, how do you like it in Eastridge so far?" His smile made her feel welcome.

"I really don't know yet. Everything is happening so fast that I haven't had a chance to think about it."

He nodded. "I know. I'm afraid Lucille has a way of pushing things on people. I hope she hasn't been too over-bearing for you. If you ever feel you're being forced into something by her, just tell me and I'll help you straighten her out. She doesn't mean to be that way, it's just her way of trying to make you feel welcomed."

"She's been very kind. I didn't mean to sound ungrateful."

"You didn't. But I know my wife, and I know how overly persuasive she can be. So like I said, if you don't know how to handle something with her, consult me. I've learned a lot about her in the past twenty-five years."

"Twenty-five years?"

"Yes, we will be celebrating our silver anniversary in a couple of weeks."

"So Lucille must have been really young when you married."

"She was. She was only sixteen. We did a lot of growing up together." His mind began to drift back in time. The next few minutes were silent as he lost himself in the past.

"How did you meet her?" She broke into his thoughts hoping to learn more about him and his past.

"I came to town trying to sell encyclopedias and asked her for directions. We started talking, and somehow one thing led to another."

"Did you sell her any encyclopedias?" Rachel teased.

His eyes twinkled as he smiled back at her. "As matter of fact, her parents did buy a set. They felt sorry for me I think. Later, her dad offered me a job in his company." He paused. "You know, that was the only set of encyclopedias I ever sold." Then he laughed, "I guess that just goes to show what kind of a salesman I was. It's a good thing I gave it up."

"So what kind of work do you do?"

"I'm half owner of a steel mill. Lucille's brother, Tom, owns the other half of the company. Her dad started me out at the bottom working as a helper in the shop, and worked me up to the assistant V.P. to the Vice President, which was Tom. Then when the old man retired, he appointed Tom as President and me as Vice President having equal ownership."

Collin burst into the room with a jovial greeting. Rae had learned already that Collin never made a quiet entrance unless he was up to some trickery. "Here's the mail, Pop. Looks like you got a letter from your prodigal son."

Collin turned to Rae, "Do you play tennis?"

"No, I'm afraid tennis wasn't real popular where I come from."

"Well, I'm getting ready to go down to the park to practice. Would you like to come along? I'll give you a few lessons."

Rae hesitated, "I—I don't think so. I'd rather just stay around here."

"Ah, come on. This is the first chance I've had to play this year, and I need someone who plays lousy to make my game look good."

Before she could finalize her refusal, Mr. Chavis looked up from the letter in his hand, the sparkle gone from his eyes. "Justin won't be able to make it home for our anniversary party. He has too many problems at the resort and can't leave." He took a deep breath and shook his head. "Your mother will be disappointed that he can't be here."

"Yes, I'm sure she will. But I'm sure my dear brother has some terrific reasons for not coming home."

Rae noticed the sarcasm in his voice and wondered why Raymond hadn't seemed to notice.

"Pop, Rachel and I are going to play some tennis." He quickly grabbed her hand and pulled her toward the door. "I'm going to teach her a few things," he added threateningly. She tried to tell him again that she didn't want to go, but he wouldn't listen to her protests. "You're gonna love tennis. It's such an invigorating sport. Gets your blood flowing and your body warm and stimulated."

By the time he'd finished talking, he already had her seated in his black Firebird and was climbing into the driver's seat.

At the park, he gave a few basic tips on how to play the game. At first she was cold towards him because of the way he'd coerced her into coming with him. *Like mother, like son.* But after a while, although she had not succeeded in hitting the ball back over the net, she found herself enjoying the challenge and becoming more relaxed than she had been since her move to Eastridge.

"Glad you came?" he hollered across the court.

"Yes, this is fun." Time slipped away quickly until she finally collapsed on the ground, physically exhausted, peacefully gazing into the blue sky. She couldn't remember playing this hard since her early childhood. Her face glowed with happiness, and her cheeks were flushed pink from the exhilarating game as Collin jogged across the court and flopped down beside her.

"You do pretty good for a beginner. With a little work on that serve, we might get a good game going."

She giggled. "I do have a lousy serve, don't I? I couldn't get that stupid ball to go over the net for anything."

Collin jumped up. "Come here."

She looked up at him pleadingly. "No, please don't make me get up yet. I don't think my legs will hold me."

"Oh, come on," and he grabbed her arm and jerked her to her feet.

"Okay! I'm coming!"

He stood behind her and placed his arms around her, showing her where to place her hand on the racket and how to throw the ball up. His nearness disturbed her. She suddenly felt flushed and warm all over. Her heart was racing, and she found it hard to concentrate on what he was telling her. Finally, to her relief, he stepped away and served the ball over the net. "Now, go get it."

Without thinking, she ran to the other side of the net to retrieve the ball. Just before she picked it up, she realized how quickly she had obeyed his orders. "Wait a minute!" She stopped with her hands on her hips and looked back at him. "What do you think I am, a dog?"

Collin was laughing as he stood waiting for her to walk back to the car with him. He whistled. "Here, Trixie, come on, girl."

She picked up the ball and threw it over his head. "Now you can fetch!" And she dashed toward the car.

On the way back to the house, she began to wonder about the way Collin had talked to his dad earlier. "I didn't know you had a brother. Is he older or younger than you?"

The bitterness returned to his voice. "Oh, don't tell me that Mother hasn't bragged to you about brother Justin yet."

"No. She hasn't mentioned him at all to me."

"Miracles never cease. Big brother is everything good and pure, just the opposite of me. He never does any wrong. I'm sure Mother will tell you all about him very soon."

She could feel a chill whenever Collin talked about his brother, and she didn't like the animosity that surfaced in him, so she changed the subject. "Your dad mentioned an anniversary party. When is that going to be?"

"Not this Friday, but next Friday night. It will be a big affair. I'm sure everyone in the city is invited. It will be the perfect opportunity for you to meet everyone."

The idea of a large party made her nervous. She had never attended anything other than a small town square dance or church picnic. She didn't know how to act at a formal party. Collin seemed to be reading her mind as he smiled and patted her hand reassuringly, "Don't worry, I'll be there. I don't care for large crowds either, but I can't let my folks down by not going. You and me will just have to stick together and help each other through it."

She felt better already. Knowing Collin would be there with her comforted her more than she wanted to admit to herself.

When they entered the house, Lucille came running from the kitchen wiping her hands on her apron. "There you two are! I was worried sick."

"Mother, what do you have to worry about? I told Dad we were going to play tennis. Didn't he tell you?"

"Yes, but you've been gone all afternoon. I didn't expect either of you would be able to play tennis this long."

"Well, you knew Rachel was with me."

"That's what I had to worry about."

"Mother," he teased. "Don't you trust me?"

"In a word? No." She said it in jest, but the worry still could be seen in her eyes when she glanced at Rachel.

CHAPTER 4

Sunday, April 22 in Eastridge

At breakfast, Raymond and Lucille invited Rachel to attend church services with them.

"Is Collin going?"

She received a look of disgust from Lucille. "Collin refuses to attend services. I just don't know what will ever become of that boy."

"You worry too much. He's still young. A lot of young people don't go to church. He'll probably change as he grows older." It was a feeble attempt to lighten the conversation.

"I don't know, Dear. Collin is too reckless. I'm afraid he may never amount to much." Lucille dismissed the discussion with a wave of her hand and changed to another subject.

After services, Lucille prepared a large dinner, and they all gathered around the table. Collin sat across from Rachel and stared at her, winking each time he caught her eye. Rachel noticed Lucille giving her husband a concerned frown. Quickly receiving her unspoken message, Raymond began the discussion. "How did the tennis match go yesterday?"

Collin laughed. "I don't think Rachel will make the all-star team. You should have seen her trying to serve the ball. It looked more like she was trying to kill flies with a fly swatter."

"Well it was her first time," his mother defended.

"Yeah, maybe with a few thousand more lessons we can actually get a game going." His words were truthful, but he said them with such malice.

Rachel tried to hide how hurt she was by his ridicule. She smiled and agreed that she would probably never be much of a tennis player. She told herself that he had just been joking around, but tears threatened to spill from her eyes anyway. Silently she scolded herself for allowing herself to feel humiliated by his attitude. It was a small thing, but her disappointment reminded her of the many times she'd seen her mother try to cover the pain caused by a male friend, only to be given away by her sad eyes.

She helped clear the table and headed for her room. Before she could get safely within the four walls, Collin's voice called her name. Half of her wanted to run, the other half wanted to face him with her wrath. In her uncertainty, she just froze in the doorway to her room. A moment later he was standing behind her.

"Hey, Rachel, how about coming with me to the bowling alley. I'm meeting a couple of friends there."

"Why? So you can make fun of my bowling too?" She blurted out as she spun around to face him.

"Uh-oh. I believe I've ruffled the lady's feathers." He gave her that fiendish grin of his. "To tell the truth, I didn't think you had so much fire in you. Up until now you've been sort of unemotional."

He reached out to her, but she backed away and slammed the door. She heard him say "Ow" and then heard Lucille's voice.

"Collin! What did you do to her?"

Rachel stood inside of the room listening to his mother reprimanding him more severely than he deserved. She could feel herself softening and was about to go to his defense when his voice interrupted Lucille's.

"Listen, Mother. I didn't do anything to her, so just SHUT UP!" She heard him run down the stairs and slam the front door.

Lucille tapped lightly on the bedroom door. "Rae, are you okay?"

Rachel opened the door. "Yes, I'm fine. I'm sorry I slammed the door so hard."

"Don't worry about it. And don't worry about Collin either. He's not worth it. I'm afraid he will always be a thorn in my side."

She was tired of hearing disapproving remarks about Collin and decided it was time someone spoke up for him instead of against him. "He's not that bad. He's just a little free-spirited."

Lucille looked distressed and turned pleadingly to Rae. "Don't be taken in by his charm. He can be so convincing at times; but I know my son. He's selfish and insensitive. To deal with him, you have to be indifferent towards him."

Rachel ventured to learn more about Justin. "I guess he and his brother are nothing alike."

The woman's face brightened as she thought of her oldest son. "You're right. Justin is very conscientious and ambitious. He's only a year and a half older than Collin, but he's already married and completely settled down with his own business."

"What kind of business?"

"He owns a ski resort in Austria."

It sounded very glamorous to Rachel, and she was impressed. "How did he ever get started in something like that?"

"He met a boy in the Navy whose family had come from Austria. He had always wanted to go back there and start a resort, so they got together after their tour of duty was over and did it."

"How often does he come home?"

Her smile was replaced with a slight pout. "I'm afraid not often enough. We're lucky if we see him once a year."

"Do you ever go visit him?"

"We've been a couple of times. The first time was to see the resort at its opening. Then last year we went back for its one-year anniversary. I couldn't believe how well they had done in their first year! That's one thing about Justin. When he puts his mind to something, he can accomplish just about anything."

"And Collin can't?"

She shrugged her shoulders. "How would I know? He's never tried to apply himself. He has no ambition or drive whatsoever. He's just a loafer. I guess he'll always be good for nothing."

Rachel had to swallow hard not to say what she was thinking. *He probably will as long as that's what everyone thinks of him.*

The spring weather had finally arrived, and Mr. and Mrs. Chavis decided to go for a Sunday drive that evening. Rachel had been invited, but she preferred to spend her evening alone. She curled up on her bed with a book from Mr. Chavis's library, but found it hard to concentrate. She felt depressed and yearned to go back home to the mountains. She wandered out to the terrace and strolled around to the front of the house. With her elbows on the railing and her chin resting on her hands, she stared upward, her thoughts as clear and empty as the light blue sky.

A door clicked open behind her and, without turning to see, she knew it was Collin. She could feel his mocking eyes on her and hoped he would go away if she didn't turn around. Instead, he came closer, without saying a word, until she could almost feel his breath at her shoulders. Finally, when she could stand it no longer, she broke the silence. "Hello, Collin."

"You must have eyes in back of your head. How could you know it was me?"

"I could feel your eyes laughing at me. What is it with you, anyway? Why do you keep looking at me that way?"

"What way?"

She turned, expecting to see his annoying smirk, but found herself looking into serious, almost sad, eyes. She couldn't speak. The accusations his mother had made about him echoed in her mind. She wanted to hold him and tell him that she had faith in him, even if his parents didn't. "I'm sorry about slamming the door on you earlier."

He reached up and rubbed his nose. "Luckily, I jumped back before my nose got smashed flat." Then he smiled slightly and eased toward her, his hands gently resting on her waist. "I'm sorry if I upset you. Am I forgiven?"

With her head lowered slightly, she peeked up at him and grinned, "Yes, you're forgiven."

"We're all alone." He pulled her closer to him and, with his finger, gently tilted her chin up toward his face, but as his lips inched closer to hers, she turned her head so that he kissed her cheek. Her face burned with warmth where he'd touched her. He smiled with a tenderness she'd never seen in him before now. "You were looking rather sad when I came out just now. What were you thinking about?"

"If I tell you, you'll just make fun of me again." She pouted playfully.

"Try me."

"I was wishing I could go back home."

He was silent for a minute as they both looked out over the front lawn.

"I'll tell you what. The Saturday following the big party, if you still feel you'd like to go, I'll take you back home. Just give me another week or so to convince you to stay. If I can't convince you by then, I'll deliver you back to your home in the mountains."

Her eyes twinkled as she looked up at him, "Would you really?"

"Sure, if that's what you want. You aren't a prisoner here you know."

"Oh, thank you!" Her arms flew around his neck as her lips lightly swept over his cheek, but before she could pull away, he had claimed her lips and was kissing her hungrily. At first she was stiff and tried to pull back, but then she surrendered to her throbbing heart and enjoyed her first real kiss. She had never allowed herself to think about what it would be like to kiss a man, but she could never have imagined she could feel so heady and disoriented over a simple kiss. A car door slammed and, when they looked down, Lucille was looking up at them. It wasn't difficult to read her expression. She was clearly displeased.

Collin shrugged. "Well, I guess I've done it again. I guarantee I have another lecture coming to me for this. She'll probably order me to stay away from you."

He straightened his shoulders and took a deep breath, then started into the house. He reminded Rachel of a small, but proud man gathering his courage to fight a larger foe, knowing he would lose the battle. Her heart went out to him. She ran back through her room and hurried down the steps only to meet Lucille half way.

"Lucille, can we talk?"

"Not right now." She determinedly walked past Rachel, dismissing her totally. "I need to talk to Collin first, if you'll excuse me." But Rachel ran after her to try to stop her from reaching Collin's room.

"Please! Lucille, I really need to talk to you right now. It'll just take a few seconds."

The older woman stopped and threw up her hands. "Okay, okay." She stomped into Rachel's room. "What is it?"

Rachel closed the door and turned to face the woman that had offered her a new life, but found herself looking into her back. "It's about Collin."

"I've warned you about him." Her voice was angry as she turned to face her, and tears were on her plump cheeks. Her anger was replaced with desperation. "Don't you understand you're going to be terribly hurt?"

"Maybe so, but don't you understand that he's crying out to be understood by you? He feels like a failure; and he will probably never be anything but a bum because you've drilled it into his head that that's what he is." She became loud with irritation. "Why don't you give him a little encouragement, for goodness sake? Stop gloating over Justin, and give Collin a little of that confidence. I've only been here for a few days, and all I've heard is what a rotten person Collin is."

At first Lucille looked ashamed, but then she composed herself and gave Rachel a sympathetic look.

"I've been hard on Collin. I admit that. But I have my reasons. Just trust me, Rae. Please don't allow yourself to get taken in by him."

She left the room, and Rachel sat on the bed in a state of confusion.

She knew Lucille was probably right. Her mother had been destroyed by men. She knew she should heed her warnings and stay clear of him. However, there was just no way that she could ignore her feelings for him.

Someone tapped on the glass door leading to the balcony. She opened it, allowing Collin to slip into her room.

"Have you seen Mother? I was surprised when she never came to my room—I wonder what she's up to—I can't believe she's not going to lecture me."

He was talking so rapidly that she couldn't get a word in to answer his question. When he finally stopped, he realized she was laughing at him. "If you'll stop talking for a second, I'll answer your question."

"What question?"

She chuckled. "You're hopeless."

"So I've been told." His nonchalant attitude had returned and so had that sassy grin that she was beginning to love.

CHAPTER 5

Monday, April 23

On Monday evening after spending half of the day at the salon getting acclimated, Rachel was having a quiet, relaxing moment alone in the study when someone drove up in front of the house blaring the horn and racing the engine. Lucille rushed into the study and excitedly told her to come with her. She allowed herself to be led through the front door and saw Raymond perched in a brand new bright red sports car, a broad smile washing over his face as he caught her eye. Lucille also beamed while she watched for Rachel's expression. Not sure what they were expecting from her, Rachel felt she had to say something.

"Nice car!" She looked from Lucille to Raymond, waiting for an explanation.

"Do you like it?" Lucille winked at her husband.

"It's beautiful. Did you trade in one of your other cars?" She wondered if Raymond was going through a mid-life crisis and wanted a sports car to make him feel younger.

"No. We just thought you could use your own transportation." Raymond climbed out of the car and handed her the keys.

Lucille chimed in, "It would be very difficult for you to get to work and your classes, when you decide to take them, without transportation. Our schedules are so hectic, we won't be able to run up and down the road to taxi you everywhere. So this is the perfect solution."

She stood in front of them feeling every emotion imaginable; excited over such a beautiful vehicle, surprised that they would do such a generous thing, relieved to be able to take the burden off of them having to drive her around, a little angry that they would assume she had decided to stay, but most of all, she was scared. The only car she had ever driven was Mr. Warren's old Plymouth to make deliveries for him, but there had been no traffic to deal with or rules of the road. Driving in the city would be a lot more difficult. "But I don't even have a license to drive!"

"You'll learn quickly, I'm sure. Most Roadsters come with a manual transmission, but we ordered this one with an automatic so it would be easier for you to learn." Mr. Chavis was smiling proudly.

"But I can't afford a car."

Lucille shook her head. "Of course you can't. The car is in my name, and it's paid for. I've always wanted a little red convertible but it's just not practical for me, so we'll just share it for now. This way you have something to drive, and I get to play with it now and then."

Rachel was speechless as she looked from Lucille to Raymond to the car. Raymond put his arm around her and pulled her toward the vehicle. "Come on, let's take a ride. I'll drive."

The week went by quickly with everyone busily pursuing their busy schedules. Lucille spent her days at the salon and her evenings cooking, cleaning, and sewing. Raymond and Collin worked at the mill, and then Raymond would spend most of his spare time reading and watching television while Collin taught Rachel to drive. After working at the salon all day, Rachel would determinedly focus on all the little details that driving involved. The mechanics of driving were a lot easier with her new little BMW compared to the old clunker of Mr. Warren's. She studied until late into the night trying to learn all the laws and rules in the driving manual. She felt an overwhelming need to be more independent. With Collin's patience and her tenacity, it only took a few days before she was ready to attempt her driver's test.

Collin drove her to the Division of Motor Vehicles and waited outside while she took her written exam, which she easily passed. Then a middle-aged, straight-faced man escorted her to her car for the behind-the-wheel test. Nerves on edge, she pulled into the traffic as he watched to be sure she did everything perfectly. Once they were on their way down the road, he no longer seemed to notice her driving ability. He was too interested in the interior and the dashboard gadgets of her fancy new sports car. He was so engrossed in them that he hadn't noticed when she missed a yield sign. When she had completed circling the block, he marked his grading chart and told her to go inside and wait for her license. She was ecstatic over her new sense of freedom.

Later, driving into the parking lot at the salon, her mood shifted to melancholy. It was only her first week, and she already dreaded going to work. Besides the sickening smell of the perm solutions, she felt uncomfortable working with other people's hair. She was convinced that working in a beauty shop was not what she wanted to do for the rest of her life. However, she didn't want to feel she were taking advantage of the Chavis's hospitality, so it seemed she had no choice for now. She walked toward the building and glanced back at the car. *Lucille's spinning her web to keep me increasingly obligated to stay.*

She ambled into the shop and began setting up her shampoo area. Beth had been cool towards her since the day she'd started working. She didn't seem to be overly friendly with anyone, but she seemed to have a special dislike for Rachel.

Milly called out, "Hi, Rae. Thank goodness you're here. We've been positively swamped, and Beth and I are the only ones working today."

Beth finished putting her customer under the hair-dryer and slithered over to Rachel. She was a tiny girl and always managed to make Rachel feel insipid and clumsy.

"Well, good evening, Rachel. How about letting me cut your hair and style it for you tonight after we slow down." She didn't voice any opinions, but her tone indicated that she disapproved strongly of Rachel's long, straight hairstyle.

"No thanks, Beth. I'd rather keep it long. It's been long ever since I can remember, and I'm kind of used to it."

"All the more reason to cut it. A new hairstyle can change your whole outlook on life."

"Beth, why don't you stop pushing her?" Milly didn't seem to have any problem standing up to Beth. "She's old enough to know how she wants to wear her own hair. Besides, I think it's too pretty to cut."

"Well, I just think that a girl that works in a beauty salon should have a more fashionable style," was her curt reply. "She looks like she's trying to be an Indian or something."

Rachel's dark eyes flashed. "I don't have to try very hard since I am Indian."

Embarrassed, Beth immediately switched to business to let the others know who was in charge. "Rachel, Mr. Milliken will be here in a few minutes. Be sure to treat him with kid gloves. He's a very prominent member of the community, and we wouldn't want him to have reason to complain."

After she left the room to go into the back office, Milly slipped across the floor and whispered to Rae. "Don't pay any attention to her. She's had a secret crush on Mr. Milliken's bank account for a long time. But so far, he hasn't even noticed her. Every time he comes in, she practically kills herself trying to get to him first." She giggled, but had to stifle it as Beth's voice addressed her.

"Milly, this isn't a social club. I suggest you get back to work."

Monroe Milliken walked through the door in time to hear the command. With her face a little more pink than usual, Beth hurried over to greet him.

"Hello, Mr. Milliken. How is the world of fashion doing?"

The man was well into his thirties, tall and pleasant looking, with short black hair, graying at the temples, and kind, hazel eyes. He was so well dressed and manicured that he reminded Rachel of models she'd seen in catalogs.

Beth led him over to Rachel. "This is Rachel. She'll be doing your shampoo while I finish with my other customer. Then I'll be right with you."

Rachel began to shampoo his hair, and it must have shown how disinterested she was in her task.

"Not too exciting, is it?"

It took a moment for her to realize that he was speaking of her job. "Uh, no, it's not. But it will have to do until I can decide just what it is I want to do with my life."

"Any ideas?"

"No, none at all. I've just been living here for a couple of weeks. I'm not even sure this city is where I belong."

The shampoo completed, she directed him to a chair in Beth's waiting area. But noticing that Milly wasn't busy, he pointed toward her chair. "The other lady doesn't seem to be helping anyone, and I'm in a bit of a hurry. Do you think she could cut my hair this time?"

Rachel glanced at Beth to see what her reaction would be, but she was concentrating so intently on her customer's hair that she hadn't heard his request. Unsure of what to say, Rachel stammered, "I - - I don't know. I understood that you were a regular customer of Beth's, but if you would prefer for Milly to…" she hesitated as she looked toward Milly, hoping for her help. Milly smiled and signaled that it would be okay.

"Okay, Mr. Milliken, that doesn't seem to be any problem at all." She directed him to Milly's chair and then went about her job, shampooing the next customer.

Rachel noticed him watching her the entire time he was having his hair cut. Before he left the shop, he walked over to her and handed her his business card. "Come by my office sometime tomorrow. I've got a business proposition that I think might interest you." He slipped out the door before she could inquire about the nature of the business.

Later, as they prepared to close for the night, Milly was overcome with excitement. "Did I see Monroe Milliken give you his business card when he left?"

"Yeah, he said he had some kind of business proposition for me."

Beth had been seething all evening and broke into their conversation venomously. "Rachel, I would like to know why you chose to give my customer to Milly. I always do Mr. Milliken's hair!"

"But he said he was in a hurry and asked if it was okay for Milly to do it since she didn't have a customer right then. I just figured I should let him have his way since you told me to give him the best service. We wouldn't want him to have any complaints about having to wait, now would we?"

She reluctantly conceded. "In that case, I guess you did the right thing. What's this about a business proposition?"

"I don't know. He just told me to come by his office tomorrow."

"Maybe he's going to offer you a job or something. He owns a fashion house, and they have fashion shows. You would make a terrific model." Milly was overflowing with glamorous expectations, but Beth was more realistic.

"I doubt that Milly. He probably has a dress that he thought would look nice on her and wants to try to sell it to her."

Rachel agreed that Beth's idea was the most logical, but her curiosity wouldn't let her sleep that night.

She stepped into the large dress shop called 'Milliken's Fashions' and was greeted by a small staunch gentleman with the stiffest and shiniest black hair she'd ever seen.

"Welcome to Milliken's. How can we help you today?" He spoke and walked in a robot fashion, making her feel anxious.

"I'm looking for Mr. Milliken's office. He is expecting me."

"Walk this way." As he led her through the shop, she had an urge to walk like a robot, obeying his order to *'walk this way'*. They entered a café where a fashion show was taking place. Models glided from table to table, letting the customers get close views of the beautiful garments. A narrator gave detailed descriptions of each one and then told its selling price, which to Rachel sounded more like prices of furniture rather than clothing.

She followed him through the café, down a short hallway, and into the offices where he left her with the receptionist.

"You must be Rachel. Mr. Milliken has been expecting you and would like you to please seat yourself at a table in the café. He will meet you there in just a moment."

Rachel retraced her steps to the tables and took a seat, realizing that Beth must have been right. He was probably going to try to sell her one of the exquisite dresses the models were displaying. *Why would he ever think I could afford one of these!* Only seconds later, Monroe Milliken joined her.

"Hello, Rachel. I'm sorry, but I didn't get your full name yesterday."

"It's Rachel Brittain."

"Okay, Rachel. Mine is Monroe Milliken, and I'd like it if you would call me Monroe for now."

"For now?"

"That's right. If you accept my offer, you will have to call me Mr. Milliken around here."

"And what is this offer?" Rachel's curiosity was increasing rapidly.

But Monroe calmly smiled and watched the platform where another model was starting her promenade. "Tell me, what do you think of my fashions?"

Rachel lifted her eyebrows. "Personally, I think they're over-priced."

It was his turn to raise his eyebrows at her straightforward answer. "At least you're honest." Then looking back at her, he came to the point. "Rachel, you're a very pretty young lady. Have you ever considered a modeling career?"

Her mind flashed back to Milly's suggestion that he might offer her a job, and her heart began to throb with expectation. "Me? A model?"

"You sound surprised."

"I am. I never even considered myself the model type. I mean, look at these girls! They're pretty and glamorous, and so sophisticated. I'm just a simple and plain girl from the mountains!"

"Wrong. You *were* a simple girl from the mountains. But now you're in the city, and you're far from plain. You're very beautiful with good height and small bones. With just a tiny bit of make-up and a little training, you could be a dynamite model. Will you think about it?"

"Do you really think I could do it?"

"I have every confidence in my choice of women. See that model coming out now?"

Rachel watched as a stunning African-American began a sensual sashay through the room. "She's beautiful!"

"Yes, she is. That's Natalie. She'll be leaving us soon to go to New York, and will probably eventually end up in Paris. She was insecure and pigeon-toed when I met her, but I knew that with a little training, she had what it would take to become a top model. And I know you can do it, too. But do you think you would like modeling clothes that are so 'over-priced'?" His hearty laughter eased her tension.

She laughed and instantly knew that she had to try it. It still seemed unreal, but she couldn't let an opportunity like this one slip past. "Okay, when do I start?"

"Next week."

"Next week!" She couldn't help wondering how Lucille would feel about her quitting her job so suddenly.

"That's right. I want you to begin your modeling career at that anniversary gathering at the Chavis' home next Friday night."

"What do you mean?"

"Come with me. I'll show you." He helped her with her chair and motioned for her to go ahead of him down the corridor to his office.

As they entered the reception area, he quickly gave his orders. "Anna, hold all of my calls for the next few minutes." Then he held his door open for Rachel to enter and closed it behind them. Pulling a sketching pad from a long, thin drawer, he showed her a drawing of an ankle-length, flowing gown. "This is my newest creation. It is done in a soft, feminine yellow with a floral print in subtle tones of green and beige. It is made right now in a size five to fit my top model; but one word from you, and I'll call right now to have it fitted for you by Friday night."

The dress was revealing at the shoulders with thin spaghetti straps. The skirt fell into tiny pleats from gathers at the base of the skin-tight bodice. A yellow, lace jacket could be added for a more complete look.

"It's gorgeous; but I've never worn anything quite so naked at the top."

"I believe you would be beautiful in it. Would you wear it for me at the party?"

She studied the picture again, trying to imagine herself in the gown. When she didn't answer immediately, he suggested, "Why don't I take you to the seamstress and see if she's finished enough of it for you to try on. Then you can make up your mind."

"Right now?"

"Unless you have something else you must do?"

"No, I don't. I'm free for the afternoon." Lucille had wanted her to go to the school to apply for classes, but she was glad to have a reason not to.

"Great! Then let's go." He grabbed his suit coat from the coat rack and led her out the door. "Anna, I'm gone for the afternoon. If anyone needs me within the next hour, I'll be at Claudette's."

Milly was waiting anxiously at the door when she arrived at the salon that evening. "Well, Rae, did you see Mr. Milliken today?"

Rachel surveyed the shop to see if Beth was around.

"Beth just went out to grab a bite to eat. Tell me! What happened?"

Playfully acting the part of an important, aristocratic snob, she announced, "You are now looking at the newest addition to Milliken's famous models." Milly squealed with delight, but stopped abruptly as they heard the door slam shut. They both turned to see Beth standing by the door, staring blankly at Rachel. She stood speechless, totally flabbergasted. Milly tried to hide her pleasure at seeing the awe-stricken expression on Beth's face, but couldn't suppress the chuckle that escaped from within her.

Beth finally found her voice. "You have got to be kidding. He actually asked you to be one of his models?"

"That's right."

"And you're actually going to do it?"

"Of course. How could I pass up such an opportunity?"

"Come on, Rachel. Do you actually think you have what it takes to be a model? No way! Besides, what about your job here?"

"I'm sure Lucille will understand. I'll talk to her tonight about my quitting. I think she already knows I've never really wanted to be a stylist." Rachel chose to ignore Beth's insulting remarks, knowing it was a result of jealousy.

Milly was overcome with the thrills of a modeling career. She babbled incessantly about the glories and expectations she had always connected with the profession. Beth remained relatively quiet, but seemed genuinely happy about Rachel's fortune after she'd recovered from her initial shock. Her attitude toward Rachel was noticeably friendlier than it had been in the past. She even invited her to take a break with her, which she had never considered doing before now.

After work, Milly walked with Rachel to her car, giving Rachel the chance to voice her bewilderment. "What on earth has gotten into Beth? She was more pleasant to me this evening than she's ever been. I thought she would be upset at my getting a job with her beloved Mr. Milliken."

"I think she might feel a little relieved that you'll be leaving the salon. Right now she's top dog, or rather 'top bitch', around here with Mrs. Chavis. Her position was threatened as long as you were working here because of your closeness with the boss."

"So that's why she disliked me so much! I never realized it had anything to do with work. I just thought she had it in for me because of my long, straight, Indian hair." She fluffed her hair and giggled.

"She's not quite *that* shallow. Don't be surprised, though, if she suddenly tries to become your best friend. Now that you'll be working closely with the richest bachelor in town, she'll be using every opportunity to use you so she can get to know him better."

Rachel glanced at her watch. "It's eight thirty. How about having a pizza with me before we head home. I'm really not quite ready to face Lucille with my news. I can figure out how I'm going to tell her while we're eating."

"Sounds good to me. I'm starved."

The house was dark and quiet when she walked in, except for the distant sound of the television in the study. She tiptoed through the family room and into the study, finding Mr. Chavis sound asleep in his recliner. She quietly crept back through the family room and stopped to gather her courage to face Lucille.

She stood in the center of the room staring at the family photographs lined up on the mantle. Lucille had been an attractive young woman, but wouldn't have been considered a beauty. She'd been blond with blue eyes and a fair complexion and had the look of a spoiled debutante, very much like Beth. She had mellowed and become more attractive with age. Mr. Chavis had also become more handsome. As a young man, he'd been very thin with dark eyes and hair. Now, with his thick silver-gray hair, he was much more distinguished. Then there were two more pictures, one of Collin, and she assumed the other one was Justin. Collin and Justin were both good-looking, yet totally different. Justin was fair with blue eyes and blond hair with features much like his mother's. Collin's eyes were also blue, but he had a beautiful olive complexion. His hair was light brown and his face was fuller and his cheekbones more square, giving him a more rugged look than his brother.

She suddenly realized that her mind was wandering, and she needed to get on with the business at hand. She quietly ascended the stairs and tapped lightly on Lucille's door, silently rehearsing her speech.

The door opened, and Lucille yawned as she invited her in.

"I'm sorry. I didn't think you would be asleep already."

"That's okay. I'm glad you woke me. At least now I know you're home, so I won't wake up in the middle of the night worrying over you."

Lucille regarded the troubled look on the young girl's face and was immediately more alert. "What's troubling you? You look so worried."

"I'm not really worried. Actually, I'm pretty excited. I just don't know how to tell you about it."

"Just come out and say it. That's generally the simplest way."

"Well, I'm sure you've noticed that I've never really been too excited over a career as a stylist."

Lucille took a deep breath and seemed to know what was coming next. "Yes, I've been expecting you would quit soon. Have you found something else that interests you?"

Her calm, motherly concern was a welcomed relief to Rachel, and her excitement now bubbled to the surface. "Oh, yes! Mr. Milliken has offered me a job as a model. And he already has given me a beautiful gown that he wants me to wear Friday night at your party. It all has happened so fast, my head is still spinning."

"Slow down," Lucille laughed. "I know it sounds glamorous, but you have a lot to consider in a modeling career. You'll have to watch those luscious desserts you love so much, and keep yourself looking nice all the time. You'll have an image to uphold in public, and the pressure can be uncomfortably intense. It's not always a glorious job."

Slowly sliding back to reality, Rachel considered her lecture carefully. "I know you're right, but I still want to try it. If I don't, I might wonder for the rest of my life what it would have been like if I had. I can always quit if I can't take the stress."

Lucille looked pleased that Rachel had found something that made her happy. "Well, at least this must mean that you are planning to stay rather than go back to the mountains." She cocked her head slightly, smiled, and seemed to be waiting for Rachel to confirm.

Rachel hesitated as the reality of the situation sunk in. "I guess I would have to stay, at least until I know if this is going to work out or not."

"Great! There's no need for you to continue working in the shop. I can get a shampoo girl. And I guess you won't be needing those classes after all."

"Well, Monroe said that I should go to what he called 'finishing school' because it would help me in my modeling as well as my personal life."

"Monroe? Is there more to this relationship than you've told me?" she teased. "I've heard that Mr. Milliken is a very charming bachelor; but he is considerably older than you."

Rachel laughed. "No, Lucille. He's a very nice man, but yes, he is a bit too old for me. Besides, I wouldn't dream of coming between him and Beth."

"Beth! Are they - -?"

"No, but she wishes they were."

"Well, she's young and still full of foolish notions. She'll realize one day that he is not available to her and set her sights a little lower."

"Gee, that wasn't so bad after all. I was afraid you would be upset with me. After everything you've done for me, then I go and quit on you."

"No indeed. I want you to be happy. Although, I have to admit, I'm a little worried about the career you've chosen for yourself. Monroe Milliken is the kind of man that a woman should be careful of. He hasn't remained a bachelor all this time for no reason. He's very attractive, generous when it suits his purposes, rich, exciting, and worst of all, persuasive."

"Okay, I'm forewarned. Don't worry." She quietly slipped out into the hall and closed the door behind her.

CHAPTER 6

Friday, May 4

Rachel carefully slipped the silken material over her head and let it slide down over her hips. The flawless pleats fell into place as she adjusted the bodice and struggled to zip the back zipper. Earlier that evening, Lucille had braided her hair on the sides and pulled it back to form a knot at the crown, leaving the back to hang in soft, flowing curls to the small of her back. Rachel looked in the mirror and couldn't believe the image looking back at her. Her naked shoulders glared at her, and she reached for the lace jacket to cover them. Then she added the tiny jade earrings and matching necklace that Monroe had suggested she wear.

She could hear voices from downstairs as Lucille and Raymond greeted the arriving guests. She slipped her feet into her heels and took another look into the mirror, gathering her courage to face the evening. There was a heavy knock on her door. Startled, her stomach and knees began to quiver.

She opened the door and saw Collin's smile fade, replaced by astonishment.

"Wow! Is that really you?"

She tried to smile, but was too tense to make it appear natural. "Oh, Collin! Do I look okay?"

"Okay! You look fantastic! I guarantee that you'll be the envy of all the other women here tonight. And I shall be the most envied escort."

"I just feel so naked. How can I go down there and face everyone as jittery as I am? Look, I can't stop shaking." She held out her trembling hands.

Collin took her fragile hands in his strong, sturdy ones and looked lovingly into her eyes. "My beautiful lady, I will be at your side the entire evening. Don't worry. Just take a deep breath, and hold your head high. You and I are going to be the most handsome couple here tonight. So relax and enjoy it."

His steady self-assurance calmed her, and she stood back to study his appearance. She had just about memorized his laughing blue eyes, of course. They had haunted her since the day she'd met him. His curly, light-brown hair encircled his tanned face like a halo. The formal white shirt, black bow-tie, and black tuxedo was inconsistent with his athletic body making him look a little awkward, but being the accepted dress for such a formal occasion, he was forced to wear it.

"Well, do I pass inspection?" he asked.

"Yes, you look very nice."

"Very nice! Not handsome? Not even mildly attractive?"

She laughed, realizing how transparent her face must have been. "Okay, I'm just not used to you like this. But, yes, you do look rather debonair; a little awkward maybe, but handsome just the same."

"Well, my dear, shall we descend the stairs in style?" He offered her his arm to escort her to meet the awaiting guests. As they marched down the steps, he remarked, "I feel like an honored subject escorting my queen to greet her court."

"Maybe you should have worn a clown suit and played the court jester instead." She chuckled and suddenly felt calmer.

They appeared very relaxed and happy as they entered the parlor. Everyone turned to see the newcomers as Lucille proudly began the introductions. The room was crowded, and as they made their way through to the other side, they discovered that people were also in the study and dining room. The kitchen seemed to be the only downstairs room that the guests had not penetrated. However, it was not a place to try to retreat due to the activity of the hired cooks and waitresses.

Rachel smiled and graciously accepted the numerous compliments on her appearance. One of the teachers she had met at the cosmetology school approached her. "Miss Brittain, that's such a lovely gown. May I ask where you purchased it?"

"It's one of Milliken's new fashions," she answered, trying to be as natural as possible.

The woman's eyes widened, and she stealthily drifted away to spread the word to the other questioning ladies. Rachel felt uncomfortable knowing their eyes were on her and that most of their tongues were wagging about her and her expensive apparel.

Monroe took her arm and led her to a chair in a remote corner. "You are doing a terrific job. That dress couldn't look lovelier on anyone else. I think you should remove the cape for a while so everyone can see the dress without it."

"But I don't feel comfortable without it."

"If you are going to be a model, you will have to get used to people looking at you. You might as well begin here. The longer you put it off, the harder it will get." In an instant, he was on the other side of the room blending in with a group of men, but watching her closely to see if she would do as he'd suggested.

She glanced around in search of Collin. When she couldn't locate him, she quickly retreated upstairs to compose herself. She removed the jacket, draped it over her arm, and checked her lipstick. Then she started back down the steps and found Collin standing at the bottom waiting for her.

"There you are. I lost you for a while, but someone said they had seen you go upstairs." He didn't seemed to notice that she'd removed the cape, and she took a deep breath trying to overcome her silly insecurities.

As the evening wore on, people spread all over the house and flowed over into the outside porch. The men were becoming rowdy from the liquor, and the women were getting giddy with wine. Collin pulled Rachel aside and leaned over to whisper to her conspiratorially, "Let's get away from here for a while. Why don't we go outside and see if we can find a nice, quiet, secluded spot."

"Sounds perfect. Let's go." The two glasses of wine she'd consumed earlier had calmed her nerves to some degree, but now that the party was growing wilder, she was becoming uncomfortable again. Collin's suggestion was heaven-sent. But as they walked arm-in-arm out of the door, they found that the entire yard was filled with more people, so they began to stroll down the road.

She had left her cape at the house, and the night air was cool on her bare shoulders. A shiver ran through her, and Collin slipped his arm around her shoulders and pulled her closer to him. "If you're cold, we can go back."

"No way! I'm not that cold. I just had a chill, that's all."

The town was practically deserted since almost everyone was at the Chavis' party. Collin stopped walking and gazed upward. "The sky is beautiful tonight." Rachel looked at the stars winking down at them. The frogs sang tenor and bass while the crickets played the lead, blending to make the most beautiful music ever composed.

When Rachel finally looked back from the stars, Collin was watching her. Their eyes met, and the rest of the world disappeared. Rachel's heart seemed to have swelled to twice its normal size as he pulled her to him. His fingers began to stroke her skin, his breathing becoming more rapid. Before she realized it, they were in each other's arms enjoying eager kisses, their hearts and souls seemingly melting into one. He began to nibble at her neck and ears, whispering to her how beautiful she was. His hands slowly roamed over her bare back sending a magical sensation through her. She slowly pulled away, breathing heavily with the desire that had consumed her. He tried to pull her back to him, but she shook her head.

"No, please, don't."

"But Rachel, I know you feel it, too. Come on."

"Not now, Collin." She looked around to see if anyone had seen them.

"You're right. This is not the best place. Someone might come by. Later?"

"That's not what I meant. I'm not ready for this."

He held her quietly for a moment. "Okay, I understand."

As they walked back towards the house, he questioned, "Do you still want me to take you back home, or have you definitely decided to stay?"

"I guess I'll stay here, but I'm not quite ready to drive so far all by myself, so I would like for you to drive me home so I can put the house up for sale and see some of my friends. I also need to clean out all of Momma's old things and pack them away."

"Okay, how about tomorrow?"

"If you don't have any other plans."

"No. Not if it means spending the day with you. Nothing can be more important than that."

Her face was glowing as they walked through the front door. Lucille immediately bustled over to greet them. She took Collin's arm and spoke quietly out of the side of her mouth. "Can I speak to you for a minute?" She led him through the foyer and into the kitchen. Rachel followed to be sure Collin didn't take all the blame for their disappearance.

"How dare you take off like that and drag Rachel away from the party. You have no right to tarnish her good name by making it appear that you've been out necking somewhere."

Rachel stepped forward to defend him. "Lucille, don't blame Collin. I needed to get away from the crowd, and he was kind enough to take me for a walk. That's all there was to it."

Clearly skeptical of the excuse, Lucille dismissed them both with a flick of her wrist. "We'll discuss this more tomorrow."

However, Rachel was not about to be snubbed. "No, we won't. There's nothing more to say about it. Besides, we won't be here tomorrow."

"What do you mean?"

"Collin is taking me back home so I can take care of some unfinished business there. I suggest that we just forget about what has happened tonight since I have already told you all there is to tell."

Lucille was taken aback by Rachel's sudden defiance. She left the room completely speechless, leaving Collin convulsive with laughter.

"I'm sorry." He tried to talk, but was having trouble controlling his hysteria. "I guess I shouldn't laugh, but I've never seen her when she was at a loss for words." And he continued to chuckle.

Rachel, recalling the stunned expression on Lucille's face, joined in his delirium. "Since I'm going to be staying here, I might as well set things straight with Lucille now, and stop letting her run my life."

Later, alone in her room, she sat on the bed and removed her shoes, wiggling her toes and massaging the ache from her ankles. She removed the earrings and necklace and massaged her sore lobes as she ambled over to the vanity. Removing the pins from her hair, she untied the plaits and rubbed her scalp, relieving the sore spots where the pins had been. Then she unzipped her dress, but stopped when she heard a tap on the glass door leading to the veranda. Knowing it would be Collin, she re-zipped the dress and slowly opened the door.

Collin stepped into the room and closed the door behind him, taking her into his arms. "I wanted to tell you goodnight. I wouldn't be able to sleep if I couldn't kiss you goodnight."

She saw the warm glow of passion in his eyes and had no doubts of his sincerity. She reached up to stroke his cheek. "My sweet Collin."

He drew her to him and let out a sigh of relief. "Oh Rachel. How did I ever get so lucky?" He nibbled at her neck causing chills to run through her entire body. The sensation she was experiencing made her oblivious to what his hands were doing until he started to unzip her dress. She shook her head 'no', and he stopped at once. The new awareness he was awakening within her surpassed anything she'd ever imagined. She had often wondered what it would feel like to be loved by a man, but she'd never thought it could feel so intoxicating. It took all of her strength to pull away from him and tell him goodnight.

Reluctantly, Collin agreed. "I'd better go back to my room and take a cold shower. I'll see you in the morning." He kissed her tenderly goodnight and quietly retreated to the balcony.

CHAPTER 7

Saturday, May 5

The trip back into the mountains was a long and emotional one. Her moods changed from minute to minute as she drove Collin completely mad.

"I just can't wait to be home again!" She longed for the familiarity of the only home she had known until only weeks ago. "But it won't be the same now that Momma is gone." Reluctance and fear of facing the pain she had been swallowing for the past few weeks squelched the excitement. She missed her mother so much, and the ache from it tortured her whenever she allowed herself to think about it. Once again, she suppressed those feelings and tried to think of only the happy memories.

Smiling, she rested her head on the headrest, feeling content. "It will be so good to see everyone. The town is so small that everyone there felt like family."

"What did you say was the name of the town?"

"Wapiti."

"Where the hell did a name like that come from?"

"Wapiti Bluff. Wapiti is the Shawnee word for elk. The mountain resembles an elk's head when looked at from far below. Legend has it that the father of all elk came from that mountain."

"We are just about half way. Are you getting hungry?" They hadn't left Eastridge until 10:30 and had packed a picnic lunch.

"Go a little further." She was leaning forward looking up the mountain. As they turned the next curve, she could see the cliff she'd been looking for. "Okay, here's a good place."

He pulled over at a small grassy knoll with a couple of picnic tables and a historical marker, an area obviously intended to be a lookout point.

She stepped from the car and pointed upward. "See, there's the elk's head."

Head tilted, Collin studied the landscape above. "I don't see anything."

"Oh, come on, use some imagination. It's difficult to see this time of year because of the thick foliage on the trees, but in the winter it's a lot more clear."

They spread their sandwiches, chips, and drinks out on one of the tables and sat down to eat. "I guess with a town name like 'Wapiti', everyone there knows of this legend?"

"Probably not everyone. Just the ones that have stopped here and read this marker about it, and those of us that had a Shawnee mother."

He stopped chewing, then swallowed and stared at her. "You mean that you are Ind....um, Native American?"

The stunned look on his face was difficult to read. Was there an air of disgust in the way he was looking at her? Or was he just surprised?

"Yes, I am half Indian. Is that a problem?"

He quickly shook his head and looked down at the table, busying himself by gathering the trash together. "No, of course not. I was just taken by surprise, that's all." He grabbed the other half of his sandwich and walked over to read the marker. It was just as she'd said. It explained the ancient Shawnee legend of the mountain. As he looked up at the over-hanging cliff, he nodded, "I guess I do see some resemblance to an animal."

She quietly joined him, pensively regarding the elk's head. "It's amazing how nature can sculpt something like that."

The rest of their trip up the mountain was a quiet one. They both had withdrawn into their own private thoughts. Apprehension gripped her as they neared her hometown.

Finally, they pulled up in front of the small cottage. Some of the perennials had already bloomed in her mother's flowerbeds. She picked a bouquet and walked across the road and through the cemetery to her mother's grave. Collin remained at the car, knowing she would want this time alone.

She knelt down and placed the flowers beside another fresh arrangement and wondered who had been so thoughtful. "Hello, Momma. I've found a whole new life in Eastridge with Mr. and Mrs. Chavis. I hope, if you're watching from heaven, that you approve of the life I'm now living. You never mentioned the Chavis's to me, but they seem to be real concerned about me, and they've done so much for me. And, Momma, I really like their son, Collin. I know if you were here, you'd like him too. He's waiting back at the house for me, so I'd better go. I love you, Momma." Tears trickled down her cheeks. She wiped them away as she stood and slowly sauntered back through the field.

Collin watched her approach. "Are you okay?"

Touched by his obvious concern, she smiled. "Yes, I'll be fine." Then she took a deep breath and tried to lighten her mood. "Well, shall we go in and begin cleaning up the place?"

They cleaned out all the dishes and kitchen utensils, placing everything in boxes. Then Collin began cleaning the refrigerator and throwing out the old spoiled food. After gathering all the trash he could, he took it out to burn. While he was doing that, Rachel busied herself with cleaning out the clothes and her mother's other belongings.

Removing the last of her mother's worn clothing from the bureau drawers caused some papers to fall to the floor. They had been wrapped in an old piece of cloth that appeared to have once been a baby blanket. She sat on the floor and began to sort through them. There was her birth certificate, which she put aside to keep, along with some old photographs of her as a child. She unfolded a newspaper clipping. It was a picture of a young man whose face looked terribly familiar. Her eyes fell to the caption beneath it as she stared in awe at the faded print: 'Raymond T. Chavis of Eastridge'. He appeared to have been in his twenties when the photograph had been taken. She recalled the picture that had been on the mantle in the family room. He had been very serious in that one, but in this black and white news photo, he looked extremely handsome, with a smile that could charm a snake.

She thought of how he looked now and couldn't believe the change. He looked so happy and carefree in this picture. But now he was quiet and only grinned occasionally, and then it was only a half smile. Something must have happened to take that light from his eyes that had once been an attractive element in his appearance. Why had her mother kept a newspaper clipping of Mr. Chavis?

She placed it in her 'to keep' pile and picked up an envelope. It was addressed to her mother, and the postmark was Eastridge. She began to open it, but hesitated as an overpowering foreboding closed in on her. She felt as if she were prying into her mother's privacy, but she also sensed there was something important in that letter that she should know. Why else would it be so carefully preserved along with her birth certificate and other memorabilia? She snatched it up and quickly unfolded it, her heart racing as an unexplained fear gripped her from within.

'Dear Jessie,

I'm truly sorry about this mess I've gotten you into. I do wish it could be different. I didn't want it to turn out like this, but now that it has, I don't know what to do about it.

I love Lucille and feel that she needs me more now than ever. I've told her everything about us, and she agrees that if you ever need money, you can feel free to call on us. She's a very understanding woman, and I feel lucky to have her in my life.

I want you to know, Jessie, that I do care about you, and I pray that everything will work out for you and our baby.

Regretfully yours,
Ray'

She stared at the letter. A faint whisper escaped from deep within. "Oh dear God." Then, the reality of what she had read seized her soul, and her heart began to pound as if it were breaking. "No! It can't be true! Please, God, No!"

Collin had entered the room just in time to hear her pleading and hurried over to her. "What is it, Rachel?"

She couldn't speak. She just stared at him with a look of shock and pain that frightened him. Then she handed him the letter, along with the newspaper clipping. She wanted to cry, but felt too numb from the shock. All she could do was watch as he read the letter and examined the clipping.

He looked up, his eyes searching her face in hope of some comforting explanation. But they both knew the truth they now had to face, and her tears finally began to flow. She started to tremble uncontrollably, and Collin ran from the room trying to escape the reality. She heard the front door slam and the car engine roar. Tires screeched as he sped away.

She continued to sit on the floor, unable to stand on her shaking legs, crying until there was nothing left inside of her except a dull ache. The truth rang through her head repeatedly: *Raymond Chavis is my father, and Collin is my half-brother.*

The room began to spin, and everything drifted into the distance. Her stomach was nauseous, and her head throbbed.

She was cold and shivered convulsively. Someone was slapping her face, and she moaned from the stinging pain. Opening her eyes, she focused on the person hovering over her. It was old Mr. Warren from the general store.

"Rachel, can you hear me? Rachel?"

She could hear him, but he seemed to be a long way away. She couldn't make herself talk; she just wanted to go to sleep. He lifted a cup to her lips and tried to get her to drink some water. She sipped a little and coughed as it trickled down her tightened throat. She sat up slowly, and he wiped her forehead with a cool, damp rag.

"I'm okay." She tried to get to her feet, but was too shaky to stand on her own. "What are you doing here?"

He helped her to the bed and propped her head with the pillows. "I saw you come into town with that young man in that black car. When I saw him speed away without you, I figured you'd had a spat. But after a while, I got worried and decided to come over to see about you. What happened? Did he hurt you?"

"No, nothing happened. I just passed out, I guess."

"But why did that young man leave the way he did?"

"He was upset." She let her head fall back against the pillows as she stared at the ceiling, remembering the reason for Collin's sudden departure. She didn't want to remember, so she closed her eyes to try to block it out. When she re-opened them, Ed Warren was still sitting patiently, awaiting an explanation. Instead of pursuing the subject, she tried to change it.

"What's been happening around here since I left?"

"Humph! Nothing ever happens around here. The biggest thing that's took place is when you up and left with Lucille. Was that one of her boys in that sporty car?"

She nodded.

A motor slowed down in front of the cottage and stopped. She knew by the loud rumbling engine that it had to be Collin returning. She was relieved that he'd come back and hadn't had an accident. She introduced the two men and then looked back to Collin. "Are you okay?"

"Yeah, I guess." He paced the room, waiting for the old man to leave.

Noticing the tense silence, Mr. Warren began to make his way slowly out of the room.

"Thank you, Mr. Warren, for helping me."

"I'm just glad I came when I did. I just had a funny feeling that something might be wrong."

Collin suddenly realized that something must have happened while he was out racing through the hills. "Why, what happened here?"

"Rachel passed out. I found her lying on the floor out like a light. She really had me scared there for a while." Then he recalled something he needed to tell her. "Oh, there is one more thing that has happened that I should mention. A Mr. Jamison came through town and was asking about you."

She frowned as she mulled over the name. "Mr. Jamison? I don't believe I know anyone by that name."

"He's an elderly man about my age and says he met you the day your mother was buried. He didn't know your name, but he knew the cottage where you lived."

"Oh, I remember him. His car had broken down, and he was trying to find the station. It was pouring down rain, so I invited him in for coffee."

"He gave me his name and phone number to give to you and wants you to call him if you decide to sell your place here. He wants a place he can come to whenever he wants to get away from the city. He's a writer or something. Says he'd like to buy the place if you won't be needing it."

She hesitated, then spoke slowly, unsure what she should do. "I was going to sell it; that's why I came here today. But now I'm not so sure. I need to think about it—but not now. I really can't think about anything right now."

"I'll be glad to call him for you and take care of all the details if you want me to. Just give me a call when you've had a chance to think about it." Then he said his good-byes and left.

The drive back to Eastridge was a tense one as they both silently languished over the fact that they were brother and sister. It was hard to know what to say to each other now. Collin stopped the car in front of the house, but he didn't turn off the engine. "You go ahead inside. I think I'll drive around for a while."

"But you've been driving all day. Aren't you tired?"

"Yeah, but I need to keep busy. I'll probably just stop and get a drink to calm me down."

"Please be careful." She reached over to touch his hand, but he drew away from her.

"Don't worry about me. I'm a survivor."

Creeping into the house, she heard voices drifting from the study. Lucille was shrieking. "But Raymond, I just don't think it is very wise for them to grow too fond of each other."

"You were the one that brought her here. What were you thinking?"

"You know very well why I did. I wanted to give you the chance to know your daughter. I felt you deserved to know each other."

Raymond Chavis spoke in a calm, soft voice. Rachel had to listen carefully to hear what he was saying. She inched closer to the study.

"I want to tell Rachel the truth."

"No."

"Damn it, Lucille! She's my daughter, and I love her. I want her to know that. I just don't like this deception."

"Do you think I do? I'm the one that got her to come here, telling her all those lies about being her mother's friend. She'll hate me for that. And then she'll probably leave. Is that what you want?"

By now, Rachel was standing in the doorway. She spoke soberly as she stepped into the room. "It's okay. I already know."

They both whirled around in surprise at the sound of her voice.

"I found a letter from - - my father," she stumbled over the foreign word, "to my mother. I also found a newspaper clipping that Momma had put away with the letter. It was a picture of you." She looked at Raymond and waited for him to acknowledge the facts.

He stood and walked towards her cautiously. "I wanted to tell you, Rachel. But I was afraid." She stood looking straight into his eyes, wanting to hate him. But the anger was gone. All she felt now was a longing to be held. Her eyes filled with tears as she broke down and reached out to him. His arms went around her easily, and he clung to her as they both wept.

He then led her to the sofa, and they all sat, each silently waiting for the other to talk first. Rachel stared at the floor, shaking her head. "There's so much I don't yet understand. Why? How did it happen?"

She had always imagined her father to be a worthless bum that had somehow taken advantage of her mother and then walked out on her. But Raymond Chavis was a respectable man, and had seemed to be one of virtue.

Lucille spoke for the first time since Rachel had entered the room. "Where's Collin?"

"He was there when I found the letter. He's pretty upset and said he was going out to have a drink. I'm a little worried about him."

"Oh, no, I've got to go find him." Lucille hurried from the room.

Raymond sat contemplating on how to start explaining the past. After an interminable silence, he spoke. "Soon after Lucille and I married, she became pregnant with Justin. We were extremely happy then."

"You really don't have to give me any explanations." She interrupted him, unsure if she wanted to hear what he had to say.

"Yes, I do. You need to know how you fit into all of this." He paused. "Like I said, we were very happy. But then I began traveling as a field superintendent for the company right before Justin was born. I was away a lot, and I happened to be away from home the night he was born. Lucille was young and frightened, and it turned out to be a long, hard birth. She never forgave me for not being there when she needed me so badly. I guess my traveling and her having a baby at such a young age was too much for her to handle. Then she became pregnant with Collin, and it was just a short time after he was born when she began drinking heavily and I realized she was an alcoholic. I loved her, but after a while I couldn't handle it any longer. I needed more stability in my life, and I needed a strong woman to stand beside me. I quit traveling and took a job within the office, but nothing seemed to help. She just kept on drinking and blaming me for it. Then I went home to visit my parents, just to get away from her." He hesitated before going on. "Your mother and I had known each other when we were kids. I enjoyed being with her and laughing about old times. She made me forget my troubles and laugh again for the first time in years. And I guess things got carried away. She was a terrific lady, and I would never have done anything to intentionally hurt her.

"Then a few months later, my folks wrote to me and mentioned that little Jessica was pregnant, and no one knew who the father was. So I went back to see her, and she admitted that I was the father." He paused again and rubbed his forehead. "By that time, Lucille had begun to realize her problems. She'd stopped drinking and was trying hard to patch up our marriage by being the best wife she knew how. We were putting our lives back together and were finding happiness with each other again. I never stopped loving Lucille, but I still cared deeply for your mother. I became terribly confused. I confessed everything to Lucille, and she took it all surprisingly well. She said that she felt she had caused it all by her drinking and understood why I had reached out to someone else.

"She became a bit upset, though, when you turned out to be a girl. She and I had both wanted a little girl for a long time. After Collin was born, the doctor had told her she wouldn't be able to carry any more children. Then, all of a sudden, I had a beautiful daughter, but I couldn't watch her grow up. Lucille made a point of meeting Jessie and keeping up with you. Through her, I was able to watch you from a distance as you grew from a baby into a lovely young lady. We sent money every now and then, especially on your birthdays and at Christmas, to help Jessie give you the things you needed."

"But why didn't Momma ever tell me any of this?"

"I don't know, really. But I don't think she ever really understood any of it enough to explain it to you, so she just tried to hide it all."

"Do you think she would be upset about me living here now that she's gone?"

"I believe she would rather you be here with people that love you than living alone in those hills."

Rachel quietly reflected on this logic, deciding he was probably right.

He stood and began to pace the floor, peeking out of the window every now and then. "I just hope Lucille finds Collin all right."

"I probably should have tried to stop him, but I don't think I could have."

"No, I doubt if you could. He never has thought much of me, but now he's going to really hate me knowing that I cheated on his mother."

"I'm really worn out. I think I'll go on to bed. Would you ask Lucille to wake me when she gets in? I want to be sure Collin gets home okay."

"Sure. You run along and get some rest."

She started out of the room, but turned back as another question crossed her mind. "Why is Lucille so hard on Collin? She must love him or she wouldn't be out looking for him."

"Yes indeed. She loves him more than anything else in this world. I've really never figured out why she's so rough on him. I think maybe she feels that he's a lot like herself and tends to have the same weaknesses that she does."

"She sure does lean on him hard."

"She's not always so bad. She's been worse lately because she was worried about you and him becoming so close, for obvious reasons."

"Yeah, I can understand that now."

She'd tried to be as strong as possible in their presence, but when she was alone in her room, she crumbled under the pressure. Her entire body fell limp onto the bed as she muffled her sobs with the pillow.

She remained awake, listening for Lucille and Collin to come back home so she could be sure he was all right. Finally, she heard them and was relieved to hear Lucille comforting him tenderly instead of scolding him. After Lucille came to her room and assured her that everything was okay, Rachel tried to get some sleep, but was unable to get her mind off of the events of the day. She stayed awake most of the night trying to sort out her situation. She was determined that she would not be a victim of life's disappointments the way her mother had been. Never again would she allow a man to touch her soul as Collin had.

She held the picture of Raymond Chavis up and studied it beside her reflection in the mirror. They were both dark with dark hair. But the resemblance was most evident in their eyes. She hadn't noticed it before, but they both had brown eyes that were shaped in the same slightly slanted way.

She entered the kitchen and found Raymond eating a bowl of cereal. He was more cheerful and wore that smile that had been so charming in the newspaper article. He seemed to look younger than he had before. She sat down and began to eat her cereal.

"Tell me, Rachel, were there any flowers on your mother's grave?"

Startled that he would know about the flowers, she clumsily dropped her spoon. "Yes. They looked fresh like they had just been placed there."

"Good." He didn't bother to elaborate any further on the subject.

"So? How did you know about the flowers?"

He shrugged, then began to explain as if she should have figured it out for herself. "Because I had asked that they be placed there, and I just wanted to be sure they had. When your mother passed away, I told the florist to send a fresh bouquet to the graveyard every month. I've been billed for the flowers, but I hadn't been able to get up there to see if they were actually being delivered."

Rachel couldn't decide how she felt about his flowers. They couldn't make up for the pain her mother had suffered because of him. She continued to eat in silence and then hurried back to her room.

She remained there most of the day, brooding about her situation. It was Sunday, a good day to hide from the world and not have to face anyone. Everyone must have understood her need to be left alone. No one bothered her all day long.

CHAPTER 8

Monday, May 7

Monday came too quickly. It was time to start living again and begin her new job at Milliken's. She showered and dressed, trying hard to focus on her new career and nothing else. For the past twenty-four hours she'd thought a lot about her future. Before her mother's death, she'd only dreamed about a life outside of Wapiti. She had never really believed it could happen for her. But now that she had experienced a small sample of what it could be like, she wanted it all. She decided that there was no way she could go back to the isolation of her hometown.

She telephoned Mr. Warren and asked him to contact the gentleman that wanted to purchase the old home place. She knew absolutely nothing about what the property was worth or how to go about getting a contract on it, and Mr. Warren seemed to be somewhat knowledgeable on the subject, so she told him to just keep her informed, but to handle everything.

She also decided to be much more careful of men. She didn't want to be totally alone for the rest of her life, but she would play it safe. There would be no more so-called 'love' in her lifetime.

When she walked into the luxurious surroundings of Milliken's and caught sight of her new boss, an interesting thought occurred to her. He was very attractive, tremendously rich, and could further her career. He would be the perfect male companion for her. Nevertheless, she also knew he was extremely astute and that she would have to play her cards very carefully.

Her first few days on the job were exciting. She was introduced to the other models and spent most of her time observing. Monroe spent a lot of time with her, pointing out each correct thing the girls did and inviting her to pick out what may need improvement. This was his way of evaluating her natural instincts for the business, and she proved herself to have a lot of promise. Her greatest obstacle would be her own insecurities. He told her that if he could build her self-confidence, she would become the most successful model he'd ever trained. He introduced her to Natalie and hoped that her influence would help accomplish this goal.

The following three weeks were hectic, the days filled with classes and the evenings spent with Monroe or Natalie either at shows or rehearsals for shows. Whenever there was a free night on the schedule, she talked him into a 'business dinner' or a 'study session'. She poured her heart and soul into her work, thereby succeeding in three of her major goals. First, she was determined to be among the best at her career. Second, she was avoiding Collin totally. However, more importantly, she was monopolizing the time of her attractive and wealthy boss, gaining his respect. She knew his work was his life and, if she could become his top model, her chances of becoming Mrs. Milliken would be greatly improved. Then she would be a highly respected icon in the community.

Finally the day came for her to begin modeling in the fashion shows. He was starting her off in a small in-store luncheon showing, introducing some of his new fall creations. Although it was only the first day of June, the fall fashions were already being introduced. In fact, they were running far behind schedule. Usually this show would have been about six weeks prior.

She arrived early, wanting to be sure she had plenty of time to fix her hair and makeup. The other models had perfected their routine so they could dress, make-up, and style their hair in a matter of minutes. But Rachel worried that nothing was going to go right for her on this first day. Her entire body was trembling, and she couldn't eat anything for the fluttering in the pit of her stomach.

Since it was a small showing, there were only four models, including herself. They would have to change quickly to keep the show going without any long delays. All the dresses were in order on the racks so they would be able to simply grab the next one as they entered the dressing room.

Rachel blotted her lipstick, hearing the music begin and the announcer welcome the guests. Panic seized her. She considered running out of the back door, never to return. *I can't possibly walk out in front of all those people without making a complete fool of myself. I'll probably fall flat on my face or something.*

One of the other girls, a beautiful tall blond, noticed her frightened expression and tried to reassure her, "You will do great, don't worry."

Rachel shook her head, "I don't know what I've been thinking. I'm not a model! I can't do this!"

But there wasn't time for doubt. Natalie, her dark skin looking beautiful and elegant in a fabulous white, tight-fitting gown, was already on her way out the door for the first promenade.

Rachel stood up and checked the mirror once more, making sure every piece of her now wavy hair was in place. She hadn't had the nerve to cut it yet, but she had curled it for the show. The second girl exited with her gown flowing behind her as Rachel quickly slid into a beautiful black and silver creation. One long, tight sleeve was silver, the other black. The colors met just above her cleavage as they crossed and became a soft drape from the undefined waist. The skirt clung to the hips and thighs, then softly flared to the floor.

When Natalie returned to the dressing room, Rachel re-checked her necklace and earrings and started out the door. She knew if she just hesitated for one second, she would back out. So she forced herself to take one step after another without any hesitation, holding her head high.

When she first entered the room, she glanced at her viewers. At the first table was Monroe, giving her a sweet smile and an encouraging nod of approval. Her confidence enhanced, she smiled as the announcer began to introduce her and her gown.

She began her stroll, her gaze falling on familiar faces. There in the center of the room was Lucille, Collin, and Raymond Chavis. *My father is here!* To her surprise, his presence made her feel a sense of pride and happiness that she hadn't expected. Just knowing he cared enough to take off from work to come see her model in her first show caused a warmth inside that she had never before experienced. She wanted more than anything for him to be proud of her.

She returned to the dressing room realizing how stiff and mechanical she must have looked. She hadn't even shown the features of the dress properly. She'd been so involved in her own thoughts, she hadn't even heard what the announcer had said.

There was no time to beat herself up for her poor performance. She would just have to do better on the next one. She quickly removed the dress, handed it to the assistant to hang, and grabbed the next outfit. This one was a suede suit in a soft rose. The blouse chosen to go with it was a darker shade of the same rose color.

Barely into the clothes, she heard her cue. Almost out the door, she realized she hadn't changed the jewelry, but luckily, the blouse had a bow that covered the necklace and did not call for additional jewelry. She hurriedly reached up and removed the earrings and fluffed her hair over her ears so no one could see her naked lobes.

This time she tried to concentrate on the announcer and showed off the details of the suit as they were explained. She kept her head held high with confidence and walked proudly among the audience. Her nerves were suddenly calmer, and she found herself enjoying the admiring stares from the on-lookers.

The remainder of the show went without a hitch, and she noticed the satisfied expression in Monroe's eyes as she took her last walk past his table. She turned just before leaving the room and gave him and the audience a slight nod. In return, he winked with that seductive smile that only he could give.

She couldn't wait to hear his reviews. She hastily changed into her street clothes and rushed from the dressing room to go find him, but standing just outside the door was her newfound family. They hugged and kissed her and told her how proud they were of her. She glanced around the room in search of Monroe, but to no avail. She accepted all their praises and congratulatory remarks graciously and thanked them each for coming, then excused herself and took off toward Monroe's office.

She found him alone, pouring Champagne into two tall, thin flutes. When she entered, he turned and offered her one of them, his eyes sparkling with admiration as he greeted her.

"You were fabulous! A bit stiff at first, but you came through." He raised his glass. "Here's to the woman who will become the most successful model in the United States, and possibly the world, if she so desires." He drank to his toast and leaned back onto his desk. "So, how did it feel?"

She walked toward him, her smiling face glowing with excitement. "It was scary at first. But after I got over the initial stage fright, it was fun!" Now she was standing within arms reach of him. She placed her glass on the desk, and then looked into his eyes with a sobered look on her face. "Monroe, I don't know how I will ever thank you for all you've done for me."

"If you continue to model and become the success that I know you can be, that will be all the thanks I need."

She leaned toward him and attempted to kiss him. She'd planned it to be a simple, friendly, thank-you kiss; one she hoped would cause him to take it a step further. Instead, he turned his cheek to her and reached for his phone, ignoring her aggressive behavior.

She picked up her glass of Champagne and slid slowly toward the window as he dialed his phone. His voice was low, but she listened carefully. "Hi...Dinner at O'Neal's?...How about 6:30. Yeah, me too. Bye." He had spoken tenderly to his 6:30 dinner date. In the weeks she had been working so closely with him, she hadn't seen him with any women, but obviously there was someone.

It was about 4:30 in the afternoon when she returned home from the showing. A strange car was in the circular drive, along with Lucille's, Collin's, and her father's. She entered the house and heard a commotion as if a party were going on in the living room. She was introduced to one of Justin's friends that had just returned from visiting him at the ski lodge. He was attractive with blond hair and a winning smile, but Rachel was in a hurry to make her apologies, change her clothes, and leave. She quickly explained that she had a 6:30 dinner date and scampered from the room and up the stairs. Once in her room, she began scheming to come up with a believable reason for being at the restaurant alone.

She entered the restaurant lobby and searched the room as casually as possible, trying to spot Monroe. She noticed a small round table in the corner that would give her a good view of almost all of the dining room and still be inconspicuous. The maître d' approached and asked if she were meeting someone.

"No, I'll be dining alone tonight and would prefer that small table in the corner, if that's okay." She gave him her most winning smile, and he graciously led her to the table she had requested.

She examined the room more closely, attempting to locate Monroe, but to no avail. Her watch read 6:25. She placed an order for iced tea and a salad with fresh fruit and settled back to await the arrival of her boss and his date. At 6:35 she began to wonder if she had the right restaurant. She motioned to the waiter and asked if there were any other O'Neal's restaurants. Just as he was about to answer, she saw Monroe walk in. She said "Never mind." and flicked her hand at him as if he were a bothersome fly.

She watched as Monroe's eyes lit up with recognition and he smiled lovingly at someone across the room. She followed him with her eyes as he walked over to a table by the window and greeted his date. The two men held hands as they talked and laughed together. She stared in awe at the two of them, letting the idea sink in. There had been no signs of Monroe being gay. She'd had no idea at all until now. At least now she knew why she hadn't seen him with any women.

Rachel swiftly finished her meal and paid her bill. Pursuing Mr. Monroe Milliken was obviously a waste of time. She would have to set her sights in another direction.

She returned home to find Justin's friend, Nathan Hamilton, still visiting. She observed his silver Porsche, his finely tailored clothing, and his obvious proper breeding. As she entered the parlor where the family was entertaining, she apologized for leaving so abruptly earlier in the evening.

"How was your hot date?" Collin's facial expression and tone disclosed his jealousy, but Rachel tried to ignore it.

"It was okay." She reached for a chocolate from the candy dish on the coffee table, but remembering her new career choice, she reluctantly pulled her hand away. She could feel Collin watching her every move. The sexual tension between them had not subsided in the least. They'd both just tried not to acknowledge its existence. Feeling it necessary to divert herself away from thoughts of Collin, she tried to concentrate on Nathan. "So Nathan, do you live around here?"

"Yes, I grew up just around the corner. Justin, Collin and I have been friends since we were little tykes."

"Really! Well you'll have to fill me in on childhood stories about my half-brothers."

Nathan laughed. "There are quite a few stories I could tell, but it may be best if I don't tell all of them. Ol' Collin has quite a colorful history."

"Oh really? I've always adored history, and I bet you could give me quite a lesson." She smiled wickedly, first at Collin, and then at Nathan.

Fearing where the conversation was leading, Lucille immediately stood up and asked if anyone would care for a drink or some coffee. Everyone opted for coffee, and Rachel accompanied Lucille into the kitchen. Lucille didn't look at her as she busied herself with the coffee cups.

"Nathan seems to be a nice guy."

"Yes, but do you have to taunt Collin like that? You know how difficult it has been for him lately."

"Yes, but it hasn't been any easier for me. What do you want me to do about it?"

Lucille turned to her and sighed. "I know dear. I'm really sorry for what you've had to go through. But all I meant was for you not to flaunt your attentions on another man in front of Collin just yet. I don't think he can handle that."

When they returned to the parlor, Collin and Nathan abruptly stopped their conversation. There was tension in the air as Collin gave Nathan a look of warning.

Nathan stood up. "I didn't realize how late it is. I'm afraid I can't stay for coffee after all. Thank you for a lovely evening, Mr. and Mrs. Chavis. And Rachel, I really enjoyed meeting you." He seemed to have trouble looking anyone in the eye and, as he was leaving, he told Collin he would talk to him later. Collin followed him to the door, and Rachel excused herself and went to her room.

It had been a long exhausting day. All she wanted was to crawl into her cozy bed and sleep.

Saturday, finally! And for once, she had absolutely nothing planned. She lounged around the house all morning by herself. Lucille had gone to the salon, and the two men had gone to the steel mill. The mail arrived just before noon, and there was a manila envelope from Mr. Warren in Wapiti. Inside was a letter explaining that Mr. Jamison had made an offer on her mother's old cottage and the contract was enclosed. She glanced over the contract, which seemed okay to her, and placed it on Raymond's desk so he could advise her what to do. Mr. Jamison had made a very generous offer of $50,000, which seemed a lot for an old run-down shack in the mountains. She considered that now she would be able to get her own apartment. She really needed to get away from Collin. Living under the same roof was becoming unbearable. She was still having trouble thinking of him as a brother.

The house was so quiet that the loud ring of the telephone startled her. "Hello, Chavis residence."

"Rachel?"

"Yes, this is Rachel."

"Nathan here. It was delightful meeting you last evening."

"Oh, hello Nathan. Yes, I enjoyed meeting you too."

"Is Collin home?"

"No, I'm afraid I have the entire house to myself."

"How lonesome for you." He sounded concerned.

"Not at all! I have thoroughly enjoyed the peace and quiet. I've done absolutely nothing except read the paper and rest all morning."

"Have you had lunch?"

"No, and I am starving! I didn't even realize how hungry I was until now."

"Would you consider allowing me to buy you lunch?"

"I'd love it. Should I meet you somewhere?"

"No. I can pick you up in about 15 minutes if that's okay?"

"Perfect! See you then."

Nathan arrived right on time. He was the consummate gentleman and seemed very self-assured as he escorted her to his car. He then drove downtown to a quaint little bistro with stucco walls, arched doorways, and tables with old newspaper clippings laminated in them. Upon entering, the aroma of freshly baked bread made one's taste buds begin to water. If you weren't hungry before you went in, the smells would arouse your appetite.

They made their way through the maze of tables. Nathan apparently knew everyone as he greeted each one or they greeted him. There was an air of friendship and warmth to the place that made everyone feel at home. He introduced her to each person he knew as they passed the tables, and she felt she were with a celebrity. Nathan was obviously well liked.

After ordering their meal, Nathan attempted to learn more about her. "So where are you from?"

"A little town in the hills."

"And what brought you to Eastridge?"

"Mrs. Chavis's car." She smiled.

They enjoyed a delightful meal with lighthearted conversation.

Later that evening as she reflected on their time together, she realized how easy it had been to be with him. There was no pressure for a relationship or any heavy decisions to make with him. He had been interesting, fun and courteous. Then she thought about her mother and how her innocent 'friendship' with Raymond Chavis had turned into a physical relationship, thus ruining her life. Men just weren't worth it!

That's when it happened. That terrible night of the fire. She'd awakened from the most horrible nightmare of her life only to find it was real.

CHAPTER 9

Sunday, June 3 — After the Fire

Rachel felt the pain on her chest, heard screams in the distance, breathing was difficult. She smelled smoke and her throat felt raw. *'Lucille!'*

She needed air. It was so dark and hot. *'Collin!'*

She couldn't find the door! Her heart was racing, fear swallowed her. The roar was deafening. *'Help!'*

In a panic, Rachel opened her eyes. Everything was white; the ceiling, the walls, the bedcovers. A TV hung high on the opposite wall, and she could hear monitors beeping a steady rhythm. She looked around, confused. Nathan rested in a chair beside her bed.

Then she remembered the horrifying fire. She vaguely remembered being brought to the hospital.

His eyes were closed. He opened them and saw her watching him. "Well, hello. You finally woke up I see. Are you feeling better?"

"My chest hurts a little." Her voice was raspy, and it was more difficult to talk than she'd expected.

"You breathed a lot of smoke. Your lungs aren't made for that kind of abuse."

"What happened, Nathan?"

"The house caught on fire. We don't know how it happened yet. The police and fire department are investigating."

"How is Lucille? And Raymond? And Collin? Was anyone hurt?" She searched his face for a hint of any expression that might tell her something.

He took her hand and spoke calmly. "Raymond is fine. He was asleep in the study but was able to escape through a window. Collin wasn't home at the time of the fire. But Lucille was burned pretty badly and is still not conscious. Raymond is with her, but they don't know if she'll make it."

Tears spilled down her cheeks as she thought of the kind-hearted woman that had taken her in and given her a new life. She wanted nothing more than to be able to thank her for everything she'd done for her. Most women would have hated the daughter who was a product of her husband's affair, but Lucille had been so accepting. She was truly an amazing human being.

Rachel sat up and tried to climb from the bed.

Nathan stopped her. "Where do you think you're going?"

"I have to see Lucille. I need to tell her how I feel. I need to be with her." Her eyes pleaded with him.

He hesitated, but saw her desperation. "Let me get a nurse and see what we can do." A few minutes later he returned with a nurse and a wheelchair. "Okay, hop in and let's take this baby for a test drive."

"Thank you." She carefully held the hospital gown together in the back while she maneuvered herself from the bed and into the chair. It was rather embarrassing to be wearing that disgusting garment, but that wasn't important right now. She just wanted to be with Lucille.

The nurse wheeled her through the corridors and into the 'Burn Trauma Unit'. Raymond sat by a bed holding onto Lucille's hand. Lucille was bandaged from head to toe and had tubes down her throat and an I.V. in her arm. Her breathing was deep and erratic. Raymond turned to look at Rachel as she approached the bedside.

"Has she gained consciousness?"

Tears filled his eyes as he nodded. "Yes, she talked to me for a while, but she's resting now." His pained expression told them that Lucille was not going to survive. He looked back at his wife and placed his hand on her bandaged forehead. "Darling, Rachel is here." The gauze wrapping did not conceal the singed hair and the fact that her eyebrows were completely gone.

Lucille opened her eyes and looked up at her.

Rachel reached out and took her hand. Knowing this might be her last chance, she spoke from her heart. "Lucille... I want you to know how much I appreciate all you've done for me. I...".

Lucille was shaking her head slowly. "Be happy, Rae.—Live a good—full life." She was hoarse, and her labored breathing made it even more challenging to get the words out, but she was determined. "That's all—thanks I need.—Take care of—your father.—He loves you dearly." Her body jerked, and she winced in pain. Then her eyes began to scan the room. "Where's Collin? -- Where's my son?"

Raymond looked at Rachel with concern. "I'm sure he'll be here soon."

However, Collin never came. Lucille's lungs and kidneys soon failed, and she passed away without telling her son how much she loved him.

Rachel pushed the food around on her breakfast tray, unable to eat. She tried to remember all that had occurred in the past thirty-six hours. She recalled being on the balcony and someone grabbing her and wrapping her in a wet blanket. And then Nathan had been by her bed at the hospital covered in soot.

"How are you feeling today?" She glanced up at Nathan peeking inside her door.

"Well, hello. I was just thinking about you."

He smiled proudly and walked toward her. "Oh yeah? I like the sound of that."

"I was just wondering if you were the one that rescued me from the fire?"

"As a matter of fact, I was."

"But I don't understand something...". She stared at the floor, frowning, as she puzzled over a small detail.

"What is it?"

She looked up at him and realized how ungrateful she must seem. "Oh, don't get me wrong. I'm extremely thankful you were there to help me, but... why were you there?"

"I'll explain all that later. Right now, I just want to know how you're doing."

"Physically I'm okay. But it's like losing my mother all over again." She felt numb. There were no more tears.

"Is there anything I can do for you?" He seemed desperate to help in some way, but she could tell he felt terribly incompetent to do so. She remembered the powerless feeling she had felt when her mother had been ill. He really didn't know enough about her past to know what she was feeling.

"You saved me from that fire! Don't you think that's enough?" Her tender smile told him how thankful she felt.

"I only did what anyone would have done in the same situation. I'm no hero. Now, do you need anything?"

"Not really. Has anyone heard from Collin yet?"

"Not that I know of. I don't even know if he knows about his mother."

"Have you seen Raym—, uh, my father, this morning?"

"No. I believe he's probably making the funeral arrangements." He glanced at his watch. "I've got to get to work. I'll check in on you again this afternoon."

"That's sweet, but I'll be okay. Don't worry about me."

He'd only been gone a short time when Collin sheepishly meandered in. He appeared to be embarrassed or ashamed. "Hi Rach. I just found out what happened."

"Where have you been?"

"I went to visit a friend out of town." He didn't look at her as he spoke. His eyes shifted from one place to another around the room without really focusing on anything as if he were extremely nervous.

She wondered if he knew about Lucille. "Have you talked to your dad?"

"No, I haven't seen him yet. I was told he had gone to the funeral home to make arrangements." Taking a deep breath, he turned away from her and toward the window.

"I'm sorry about your mother." She wanted to tell him that Lucille had asked for him, but thought that might make him feel even worse for not being there.

"Me too. I guess I should go find Dad and help him with everything." He turned back toward her. "I just wanted to see you and make sure you're okay."

"I'm fine."

He turned to leave and almost collided with Raymond as he entered the room. Again he looked ashamed and ducked his head. Raymond seemed not to notice as he grabbed a chair and pulled it toward the bed.

"Son, please stay. There's something I need to talk to you and Rachel about. Get a chair and come sit down."

Collin dragged another chair over to the bedside. Raymond sat leaning forward with his elbows on his knees and ran his fingers through his hair.

"Just before your mother passed away, she and I had a talk. It was very important to her that she confess something to me so she could rest in peace." He struggled to find the right words.

"Dad, you don't have to go into this now. It can wait." Collin started to get up, but Raymond reached out and clutched his arm.

"No, it can't, Son. The truth has been kept a secret for too long already. You and Rachel need to know what your mother had to say."

Collin and Rachel exchanged bewildered looks.

"What secret?" For the first time since he'd arrived, Collin was not fidgeting about. He was suddenly very intent on what his father had to say.

"Before I tell you, I want you to know that I had no knowledge of any of this. And no matter what problems you and I've had, I've always loved you."

"I know that Dad. What is it?" Collin was becoming frustrated and anxious.

"Well, as you know, Rachel is my daughter as a result of me cheating on your mother when you were very young. We were having serious problems in our marriage..."

"Yes, Dad, we know all of that." Collin didn't want to be reminded of the pain he'd suffered because of his father's infidelity. "So what did Mother tell you?"

"I never really understood why your mother was so forgiving about that situation. She'd been such a saint, rising above it all and going on as if it never happened. And then she'd accepted Rachel and helped me stay in touch and keep up with everything that happened in my little girl's life." He hesitated, looking lovingly at Rachel. "What I didn't know was that Lucille had been almost relieved that I'd cheated on her because it helped ease her own guilt. She'd been hiding a little indiscretion of her own. While I was away on one of my business trips, she'd had an affair." He looked at Collin and took a deep breath. "Collin, you're not my son. That's what your mother wanted you to know before she died."

Collin stared at Raymond, the man he had always called 'Dad', in disbelief. "I don't believe this. Why would Mother hide something so important?— So who is my father?"

"She wouldn't say. What she did say is that he's no longer living, and so it doesn't really matter who it was."

Collin looked at Rachel and shook his head. "This is just fuckin' incredible." His voice was almost inaudible. Still dazed, he stood up and started toward the door. "I'll see you two later. I've got to get out of here."

After he'd gone, Rachel sympathized with her father. "It must have been difficult for you to hear that after all these years of believing he was your son."

"I always felt there was some reason I couldn't relate with Collin in the same way that I could Justin. He was always just so difficult, almost like he didn't feel he belonged. No matter how hard I tried, I couldn't get through to him. But I loved him. I still will always think of him as my son." A tear trickled down his cheek, and he quickly brushed it away.

Nathan came back that evening with an armload of flowers. She had also received a beautiful bouquet from Milly, Beth, and all the girls at the hair salon, and a huge arrangement from Monroe and the other models. There was also one yellow rose with no card.

"So, how's my hero this evening?"

"Tired. It was a long day. And I'm no hero, I told you."

"I told you that you didn't need to come back here to check on me. I'm just fine. In fact, the doctor says I can leave the hospital tomorrow morning."

"I know. I just saw him in the hall, and he told me."

"The flowers are lovely." She could tell he had something on his mind, but she didn't want to push. She quietly waited for him to open up to her.

"I understand the funeral is on Wednesday. They wanted to be sure you would be able to be there, so they put it off one extra day." He seemed to be making small talk and avoiding whatever it was that was occupying his mind. "Would you like for me to take you home in the morning?"

"Thank you, but my father said he would come get me. Since we don't actually have a home to go back to, he says we'll be staying with a relative."

"Well, if you need me, I can be here."

He obviously wasn't going to voluntarily tell her what was bothering him. "What's wrong?"

"Just a lot on my mind. Nothing for you to worry about."

She wanted to tell him about what she'd learned about her father and Collin, but decided that it was best left in the family for now. "Are you sure there's nothing you want to talk about? You just look so troubled."

"No, I'm just tired. I think I'll head on home."

After he left, Rachel looked at the yellow rose and wondered who had sent it. *Yellow roses were Momma's favorite*. Having the single rose on her nightstand was comforting. It somehow made her feel that her mother was nearby.

The narrow graveled road wound through a canopy of trees, eventually opening to a breathtaking view of green grass, flowers, a flowing rocky stream, and an old renovated mill house.

"Welcome to our new home! At least, temporarily." Raymond stretched as he climbed from behind the driver's seat and stood by the car admiring the beauty of his sister-in-law's home. She'd purchased the old mill property a few years ago and remodeled it into a cozy home for herself.

Rachel gasped as she took in her surroundings. "It looks like something out of a fairy-tale."

They walked toward the doorway. The quiet and peaceful setting gave way to a jovial voice exploding from within the building as the door flew open. There stood a beaming wild-haired woman with a broom in her hand. "Come on in and make yourselves at home." She patted Raymond on his back as he walked through the door. Rachel was still standing in awe admiring the exterior of the old building. "Come on young lady. Let's get this door shut before the bugs take over my house." She shooed her through the entrance, closed the screen door and then stood looking up at Rachel. "My, my. What a beautiful girl you have here, Raymond."

"Rachel, this is Martha Shaw, Lucille's sister, who has been generous enough to offer us a place to stay until our home can be rebuilt."

The grizzly woman shooed him away. "Raymond, no one has called be 'Martha' since I was a kid. Sweetie, I'm Aunt Marty to you, just as I've always been to Justin and Collin."

Wonderful aromas of home-baked goodies filled the air as Rachel looked around her quaint surroundings. There was nothing fancy or expensive, or even matching, about the furnishings. In fact, it would have been an interior designer's nightmare. Nevertheless, the room was warm and inviting with its over-stuffed chairs and sofa with afghans thrown over them. The old pine end tables were covered with well-used crocheted scarves. The dark stained wood floor was covered with oval braided rugs in the small living area and hallway. "What a wonderful place. It feels so much like home." She suddenly realized how much she had missed her home. There was even an old wood stove in the corner of the room exactly like the one she fondly remembered warming herself by as a child. Her smile was heartfelt when she turned back to Aunt Marty. "Thank you so much for letting us stay here. I hope we're not imposing too much."

"Oh, not at all! This place could use a little more activity. It can get pretty lonesome around here. By the way, where's Collin?"

Rachel had been wondering the same thing. She hadn't seen or heard from Collin since they'd been told that they were not brother and sister. She wondered what he was feeling toward her now.

Raymond looked worried. "I don't know where he is. I haven't heard from him since I told him."

"Poor boy." Aunt Marty shook her head at the floor. "I told Lucille all those years ago that this would happen one day. But she wouldn't listen. She never listened." She was still staring at the floor, almost in a trance.

Raymond looked at Rachel and quietly signaled for her to follow him. They started down the short hallway and heard Aunt Marty as she began to putter around, sweeping, straightening, and muttering to herself.

He led her up the old rickety wooden stairs to a loft bedroom. It was small, but had the basic necessities; an old mahogany vanity, a chest-of-drawers, and a bed. Thinly worn area rugs covered the floor between the furnishings. There was a small night table with a little milk-glass lamp beside the bed. There was one small window in the corner of the room that opened to the sound of the babbling stream. She could barely see the edge of the water wheel if she looked down and to the left.

"We weren't able to save much out of the fire, but there are a few clothes in the drawers that people have sent to us. The town has really rallied to help us out. Make a list of things you need, and we can go shopping later." He started to leave, then hesitated. "I'm sure you'll need something to wear to the funeral, so I guess we should get to the shopping center tonight. The service is in the morning at ten o'clock."

The funeral service was a simple one. The church auditorium overflowed as everyone in the town came to pay their respects. Milly and Beth were there, along with the rest of the employees from the salon. Justin had flown in from Austria and arrived just before the services began.

Across the street from the church, Rachel noticed a white van with "WWAC TV NEWS" painted on the side. News crews had set up their cameras and were filming the funeral.

The family left the church to walk over to the cemetery and was greeted by a swarm of well-wishers that had been unable to get into the chapel. Rachel hadn't seen Collin during the service, but now noticed him standing by a tree at the edge of the cemetery, just watching.

The crowd was beginning to disperse so she turned to go to him, but was detained by Raymond introducing her to Justin.

"Rachel, this is your half-brother, Justin."

Justin reached as if to shake her hand, but after grasping it, pulled her toward him and gave her a warm and hearty hug. "Mother and Dad's letters were full of praise about their beautiful new daughter, and I see they didn't exaggerate."

"Did your wife come with you?"

"No, she had to stay behind and run the lodge. In fact, I can't stay. I'm heading back to the airport in a few minutes. You will have to come out for a visit soon so we can get better acquainted, Sis."

Other friends and acquaintances surrounded them, drawing Justin's attention away from her. She slipped from the crowd and looked again toward the tree where Collin had been, but he'd disappeared. Nathan emerged from a small gathering and came to her side as she was trying to see where Collin had gone. "What are you looking for?"

"I saw Collin over by that tree earlier. Do you know where he went?"

"No, I haven't seen him." He didn't seem concerned. In fact, he almost looked disgusted or angry.

"What is it, Nathan?"

"What?"

"This problem you seem to have with Collin?"

"Let's not talk about that now. This isn't the time or place."

She glanced around at the departing mourners and agreed. "But I do want to discuss this later." She wouldn't let him off the hook. There was something very strange about the way he'd been acting.

CHAPTER 10

Thursday, June 7

Rachel rubbed the sleep from her eyes as she walked through the hallway toward the kitchen enjoying the wonderful aroma of freshly perked coffee. She was startled awake as her bare feet stepped onto the cold, damp cobblestones that had been part of the original floor of the old mill. *The air-conditioning is certainly doing its job in this old building!*

Aunt Marty and Raymond were sitting at the small wood-plank table. Bran muffins were waiting for her on the stove. Aunt Marty scampered from the room and returned with a pair of socks, which she tossed to Rachel.

"Thanks!" Her feet welcomed the warmth as she smoothed the thick soft fabric over her frozen toes.

They were finishing their breakfast when there was a knock on the front door. A man identified himself as a detective for the insurance company that had insured the Chavis' home. "Well don't just stand there, young man. Come in here and shut the door." Rachel had already learned that Aunt Marty knew no strangers. Everyone was treated as a member of the family. The older woman indicated the chairs in the living room, and everyone gathered around to hear what the investigator had found out.

"Mr. Chavis, there is no doubt that this was arson. I do have a few questions that I'm hoping you can answer for me."

Raymond was still stuck on the word 'arson'. "Who would do something like that? And why?"

"We haven't narrowed that down yet, but we are working with the local police, and they have a few leads." Before anyone could respond, he continued. "Mr. Chavis, why were your smoke detectors disconnected?"

Raymond thought for a moment. "We disconnected them when we had the anniversary party because of all the smoke from the cigarettes. I guess we forgot to connect them back after the party." He rubbed his hands over his face and was noticeably guilt-ridden.

The detective shook his head. "I wish people would get it through their heads that they should never disconnect the alarms." He instantly realized how insensitive he had been and sheepishly glanced up at Raymond. "I'm sorry."

There was an uncomfortable silence.

Aunt Marty stood. "I think I'll get me some coffee. Would anyone else like some?"

Everyone declined the offer.

Raymond needed to know more. "What else have you found out?"

"Well, we know the fire originated in the kitchen. A combustible liquid, probably gasoline or kerosene, appears to have been poured onto the kitchen floor and ignited. The fire spread quickly through the rear portion of the house, completely destroying the kitchen, study, stairway, and upstairs rear bedrooms. The front foyer, parlor, dining room, and upstairs front bedrooms are still intact, but badly charred. Have you contacted any contractors yet?"

"Yes, I've talked to Nathan Hamilton. He's one of the best in the area and a friend of the family. I would like for him to do the work, if that's okay with you?"

"Well, we usually require at least two estimates. But if he is in line with our assessment, there should be no problem." He began writing in his notebook. "What is the name of his company?"

"H & J Construction. Hamilton & Jennings. Frank Jennings is his partner."

Nathan had mentioned to Rachel that he worked in construction, but she had assumed that he was only an employee or that his family owned the business. She was surprised to hear that he owned his own business at such a young age.

The investigator was continuing. "Now, I understand you have a son," he consulted his notes, "Collin?"

"Yes."

"Is he around by any chance?" He glanced around as if expecting to see Collin materialize.

Raymond looked at Rachel and Aunt Marty, and both of them shook their heads. "No one has seen him much since the fire. Losing his mother has been very difficult for him."

"Of course." The detective was glancing through his notebook. "Was your son at the funeral?"

When Raymond hesitated and looked uncomfortable, Rachel spoke up. "Yes. I saw him briefly at the cemetery." Raymond looked at her, but didn't ask any questions.

The detective turned his attention to her. "Are you sure? No one else seems to remember seeing him there."

"Yes, I'm sure. He stood away from the crowd. I could tell he was just too overwrought to face anyone."

"I see." He studied her skeptically, and then turned back to Raymond. "Did you see your son there?"

"I didn't notice who was there and who wasn't. I was kind of numb through the whole service. I was just concentrating on getting through the nightmare of it all."

For the first time, the investigator showed a faint flicker of compassion. "I understand. I'm sorry I have to ask these questions, but it's the only way we can find out who did this horrible thing."

Aunt Marty exploded. "Well, you certainly aren't going to sit there and say you think Collin did this, are you?"

Before he could respond, there was another rap on the front door. Everyone listened as Aunt Marty invited the new arrival to join them in the living room.

The uniformed officer addressed Aunt Marty. "I'm sorry to have to intrude on you like this, Mayor, but it is important."

Rachel's jaw dropped open. Mayor! She just couldn't imagine Aunt Marty as a mayor.

"Don't be silly, Sheriff. What can I help you with?"

The insurance investigator stood and shook hands with the sheriff. "Good to see you again, sir. I was just asking Mr. Chavis a few questions."

The sheriff didn't look impressed and turned back to Aunt Marty. "Is your nephew, Collin, anywhere around here?"

Aunt Marty stepped back and gave the officer an incredulous stare. "Not you too, Sheriff. You can't possibly believe that Collin had anything to do with that fire."

"I'm sorry, Mayor, but so far all the evidence is pointing straight at him."

"What evidence?"

He smiled. "You know I can't divulge that information, Marty. But the investigation is still on-going and, all I want right now is to ask Collin a few questions. Hopefully he can clear everything up."

"As we were just explaining to this other gentleman, none of us has seen or heard from Collin since the funeral. He just needs some time alone to grieve. I'm sure we'll hear from him soon."

"When you do, please be sure to notify us. We would like to resolve this as soon as possible."

"Of course. Now if both of you gentlemen don't mind, we would like to get on with our day." Aunt Marty walked to the front door, indicating it was time for them to leave. Rachel couldn't help smiling at the woman's candid demeanor. The two visitors heeded their cue and left the house like scolded puppies.

"The nerve of those two to actually think my nephew could do such a thing! Really!" She continued muttering as she proceeded to the kitchen to clean up the breakfast mess.

Rachel suddenly realized she'd sat through the interrogations in her robe and socks with no makeup and her hair a total disaster. She glanced at the clock and dashed to her room to dress for work.

After a hectic two days both at work and at home, with the media hounding the family members and setting up camp on the outskirts of Aunt Marty's property, Rachel welcomed a quiet Saturday behind closed doors. Since the news had broken that the fire had been a case of arson, it had become a major headline in this small quaint city.

Nathan offered to take her out for a relaxing dinner, and she gladly accepted. Not only could she use a night out, but she also had a lot of questions for him. Every time she'd asked him anything about the night of the fire he had sidestepped, changing the subject or putting the conversation off for another time. Well, that time was here. She needed answers.

After using evasive tactics to avoid the media frenzy, they finally sat alone in a secluded corner booth in the dimly lit Italian restaurant. A small candle flickered in a round red jar in the center of the table. The waitress placed their enormous meals in front of them while Rachel waited for her chance to start her inquisition. The waitress left, and she watched as Nathan began to chop at his food.

"So, is now a good time to answer all those questions you have been avoiding?"

He never looked up, but continued to fill his mouth with the stringy spaghetti. "What questions?"

She began twisting her fork through her spaghetti. "What inspired you to be at the house the night of the fire? I mean, how did you just happen to be there to come to my rescue?"

He stopped eating and sat back, resigning himself to the fact that it was time to tell her what she needed to know. "That was the night you and I had been out to dinner together."

"Yes, I remember." She waited.

"Well, when I got home, Collin was there waiting for me. He said we needed to talk. He was really in a bad way. I don't know for sure, but I think he'd been drinking. He was so depressed and angry."

"Angry? With you?"

"With me, you, his parents, the world. He started by threatening me, saying I had better stay away from you. Then he just started whining about how his life sucked. I got him to sit down and have some coffee with me and just let him talk everything out. He told me about how he'd fallen in love with you and then found out how his father had cheated on his mother, making you his half-sister. Then he started talking about his jealousy of his brother, Justin, and how his mother and father adored him and hated Collin and probably wished he had never been born. The more he talked, the more angry he became, until he finally ran out of my house saying how he would show everybody. I thought about what he'd said all evening and became worried about what he might do. So I decided to drive over and make sure everything was okay. That's when I saw the flames and heard you calling out for help."

None of his story was really surprising to Rachel, but hearing it made her begin to wonder. "Do you think that he could have set the fire, Nathan?"

He shrugged. "I don't know. I don't want to believe it, but not only was he in a rotten state of mind that night, but he hasn't acted right since. Of course, he did lose his mother in that fire. I guess that could explain the way he's acting."

"Of course it could. Losing your mother is very devastating. It makes you feel abandoned and empty. I still feel that void inside of me. I don't think it will ever go away." She was quiet as she thought about her own mother. Losing Lucille had increased the size of the abyss within her.

"I'm sorry. I guess you would know how Collin is feeling, if anyone does."

She took a deep breath and shook off the gloom that was penetrating their conversation. "Okay, so that explains why you were in the right place at the right time. Thank God. If you hadn't shown up when you did, I probably would have jumped off that balcony and killed myself." Again, she thought of poor Lucille.

"Don't think about that now. How's your spaghetti?"

"Good. So tell me, is that the reason you've been so angry, or whatever it is you've felt toward Collin? I've noticed some kind of animosity in you whenever I mention him."

"Yeah, I guess I really think he could have done it. He just seemed like, in his state of mind that night, he was capable of just about anything."

"I hope you're wrong. I just can't imagine him doing something like that. Not the Collin I know." She was anxious to change the subject. "I understand you're going to rebuild the Chavis' home?"

"Yeah, we've already begun the demolition of what was left."

"You're going to tear down the whole house?"

"It's actually cheaper to tear it down and start over than to try to reinforce the scorched areas and build around it. There was just too much damage to the structural integrity of the building."

"Will you build it exactly like it was?"

"That's up to Mr. Chavis. I'll build whatever he wants. He's considering building a smaller house, but I don't think he's decided what to do yet."

"But the house was so beautiful. I wish he would just let you build it back the way it was."

"I wish he would, too. I'd sure enjoy building a house like that. That's the kind of challenge all contractors love to tackle."

CHAPTER 11

Sunday, June 10

Collin and the events of that awful night stayed on her mind as she tossed and turned all night, trying desperately to put it out of her mind so she could get some sleep. It was the wee hours of the morning before she gave in to exhaustion.

She awoke to a beautiful Sunday afternoon and decided to take a drive to the Chavis' property to see how things were progressing with the leveling of what remained of the destroyed home. She parked the car and walked among the debris, trying to ignore the spying reporter that followed her and now watched from a half block away.

An intense lump gripped her from deep within herself until her entire body began trembling, and she burst into sobs, tears streaming down her face. She fell to her knees and let herself mourn. She grieved for her mother, for Lucille, for her lost childhood, and for the pain the Chavis's had to endure due to the loss of their home and the destruction of their family. She looked up to the sky and prayed for each of them. Then she stood slowly, completely spent, and looked around at the ruins once again.

She wandered toward the rear of the house and kicked aside some of the ashes. She noticed a metal cookie sheet and picked it up. It was covered in soot, so she threw it back down and started to turn to walk away when she saw a glimmer. She looked more closely and saw the sun reflecting off of something in the ashes. She bent down and retrieved a chain with a diamond ring on it. Stuffing it into her pocket, she looked around once again at the ruins.

A dump truck and a bulldozer sat deserted, waiting to begin the final demolition the next day. Something moved near the truck. She crept toward it. Collin appeared from the shadows, wandering almost aimlessly toward her and the destruction. He saw her, but seemed almost paralyzed by anguish.
"Hello, Collin."

He nodded slightly, looking around at the rubble. "Mother didn't deserve to die like that." He shook his head. "It's just as well that the house is gone. It wouldn't be home without her anyway." He looked at the sky and then at Rachel. "How's Dad doing?"

"He's coping. But he's worried about you. Everyone is."

"I'm okay. I had a lot to sort out and did a lot of thinking. But now it's time for me to pull myself together and join the world of the living again. Tell Dad I'll be back at work tomorrow."

"Why don't you come back to Aunt Marty's with me and tell him yourself. He would love to see you."

A half smile touched his lips, and he looked grateful for the invitation. "Good old Aunt Marty! How the hell is the old broad?"

"Quite a character, I'd say."

Collin put his arm around her shoulders, and they walked together toward her car.

"I see H & J's equipment is ready to go to work. Is Heckle & Jeckle going to rebuild the house?"

"Heckle & Jeckle?"

He smiled, though sadness still showed in his eyes. "It's an old joke around here. When Nathan and Frank first went into business, we teased them about not knowing anything about the building business. When they named the company H & J Construction, we used to tease them by calling it Heckle & Jeckle Construction."

She looked confused. "I don't understand."

"Heckle & Jeckle? A couple of cartoon characters?" He realized that she'd never heard of them and started to explain, but changed his mind as he realized how ridiculous the whole thing seemed now. "Never mind, it's not important."

Rachel had only driven a few blocks when they met a deputy's car traveling toward them. The deputy recognized Collin in the passenger's seat and performed an immediate U-turn with lights and siren blasting, announcing to the world that he had found his man.

Collin looked around at the pursuing vehicle and then at Rachel's speedometer. "What's he chasing you for?"

Rachel proceeded to pull to the side of the road. "They've been looking for you."

"For me? What for?" There was genuine surprise in his voice and on his face.

"They said they want to question you about the night of the fire." She didn't have time to explain anything further as the deputy cautiously approached her window.

"Please turn off your engine and remove the keys from the ignition."

She did as she was told. The deputy stood close to the car, behind her so that the door couldn't hit him if she chose to open it. He was being extremely cautious, treating the situation as if they were dangerous criminals. He kept one hand at his side near his gun and reached toward her window with the other.

"Please hand me the keys."

She did.

"Now place both hands on the steering wheel where I can see them, and do not remove them."

She was becoming very nervous, but continued to do as she was ordered.

Collin was getting agitated at the way she was being treated. "What is this all about? There's no reason for all this drama, for God's sake!"

The deputy became defensive and his voice amplified. "Sir, please step slowly from the car with both hands in plain sight."

"What's this 'sir' stuff, Rudie? You and I have known each other most of our lives. We went to school together and played ball together for Christ's sake." He had stepped out of the car and was beginning to walk around the car as he talked.

"Collin, stop where you are, and place your hands on the car." Rudie maintained his judicial manner.

Collin shook his head in disgust, but obeyed the orders. "What is this all about?"

Rudie was a rookie cop and took his job very seriously. As far as he was concerned, this was a major bust, his first since he'd joined the force. It didn't matter that he had been friends with the perpetrator in the past. All that mattered was that Collin was now a suspect in a felony, and Rudie was excited to be the one to find him.

The reporter that had been tailing her had parked his car and was rushing to take pictures of Collin being arrested. Rudie tried to make him leave, but he quoted his 'right to free press' and continued taking pictures.

Once Collin had been cuffed and placed in the rear of the police car, Rudie returned to Rachel. "Could I see your driver's license and registration please?"

She reached for her purse and removed the items from her wallet, handing them to him.

"Miss Brittain, where were you headed when I stopped you?"

She remembered quickly about Aunt Marty being the mayor. "To Mayor Shaw's house, where I'm staying temporarily until our house is rebuilt."

"Did you realize that you were harboring a fugitive?"

"I wasn't 'harboring' anybody. I was just giving him a ride to his Aunt Marty's. Besides which, I understood from the sheriff that he was only wanted for questioning. That doesn't make him a 'fugitive'."

Satisfied that her intent had been innocent, he returned her keys to her and told her she was free to go.

"Would it be all right if I follow you to the station?"

"There is no need for you to do that, Ma'am."

"That's not what I asked. Would it be all right if I do?"

"Sure, if that's what you want." He shrugged his shoulders and walked back to his vehicle.

As they approached the police station, she noticed a pay phone just outside the building. She parked her car, phoned Aunt Marty, then went inside.

She'd expected a noisy, bustling department like she'd seen on television programs, but what she found was an empty and quiet reception area with one officer sitting behind a desk. The only other person in the room was the reporter who had been standing back waiting for his chance to pounce as soon as she entered.

"Miss Brittain, can you tell me what you know about what happened the night of the fire?"

She stared at him in disbelief, shook her head, and pushed pass him to approach the reception desk.

"Can I help you, young lady?" The officer looked bored and disgusted with the reporter.

"I hope so. An officer just brought Collin Chavis in for questioning. Where would I find them?"

"They're probably in the interrogation room. You wouldn't be allowed in there unless you're his attorney."

"Could I see the sheriff, then?"

"The sheriff is probably helping with the interrogation, but I will check. What's your name?"

"Rachel Brittain."

He reached for his phone and pressed a few buttons. "There's a Miss Rachel Brittain here to see the sheriff." There was a long pause. "Okay." He hung up the phone and stood up, walking around the desk and grabbing a huge ring of keys from a clip on the side of his belt. "This way."

The reporter tried to follow at their heels, but the officer explained to him that he was not allowed to go in. He unlocked a heavy steel door and led her through a short hallway and into a large room with several cubicles. A small sign over the entrance said 'Investigations'. There were a few chairs lined up along one wall. "You can have a seat, and the sheriff will be with you as soon as he's finished with the interrogation."

"Thank you. When Mayor Shaw arrives, would you kindly show her where to find me?"

Suddenly he didn't look as bored with her as he had before. He looked straight at her with clear, alert eyes and gave her a slight smile. "Yes Ma'am, of course." It was apparent that Aunt Marty was highly respected by her peers.

About twenty minutes had passed when a door opened about ten feet from where she was seated. She couldn't see inside the room, but she heard Collin's voice. "I don't know; all I know is that I didn't do it."

Officer 'Rudie' came through the door and strutted over to a table in the corner that held a coffee-maker and cups. He poured two cups and disappeared back through the door, closing it behind him.

Just then, a whirlwind of commotion erupted from the hallway. Aunt Marty burst into the room, along with the officer from the front desk and another gentleman with a briefcase. "Where is my nephew?" She charged through the door to the room where Officer 'Rudie' had taken the coffee. "What do you think you're doing questioning him without his attorney present? Collin, did they tell you your rights?" The man with the briefcase followed her into the room. The door closed behind them, and Rachel was left alone, waiting.

The room must have been soundproof. When the door was shut, everything was completely silent. Yet, whenever someone came in or out, there was an eruption of loud voices emanating from within.

Raymond was shown through the hallway by the same front desk officer. "Rachel, what are you doing here?" He sat down beside her as the officer headed back out the door.

"I was with Collin when they brought him in."

"Where is he now?"

"In there." She indicated the doorway. "Aunt Marty and the sheriff are in there, along with Rudie and a man with a briefcase. I assume he's an attorney."

"How long have they been in there?"

"Collin and the sheriff have been in there close to an hour. I guess Aunt Marty and the attorney got here about fifteen or twenty minutes ago."

The door opened, and Rudie had Collin by the arm leading him out, handcuffed behind his back.

Aunt Marty came next. "Don't worry, son, they don't have enough to hold you. We'll have you out in no time."

The sheriff came out, rubbing his hand over his face as if it had been a difficult and painful experience.

The attorney followed him, briefcase in tow. "I'll be back as soon as I've spoken with the judge. You had better have a lot more evidence than this circumstantial bull if you plan on keeping him in jail." He stepped briskly past everyone and hurried down the hall.

Collin had already been escorted away to a cell. Aunt Marty joined Raymond and Rachel. "This is ridiculous. They are so anxious to blame someone for this crime, they don't even care if it's the right person or not."

The defense attorney was unable to get a bond hearing until the following morning. At that time, the prosecuting attorney presented a stronger case than any of them had expected. Although Collin claimed to have been with Nathan that evening, the prosecution said that his alibi had holes in it. Therefore, they felt that there was opportunity.

They professed to have evidence collected from Collin's place of employment that pointed to his guilt and witnesses that would testify to his motives. Collin's reputation as a troublemaker did not facilitate his defense at all. In the end, his bail was set at $300,000, and a trial date was set for Monday, June 25th.

Rachel left the courthouse feeling confused. She was having a hard time believing that Collin could do such a horrendous act, but the evidence was certainly pointing his way. *Could Lucille have known a darker side of Collin? Is that why she'd been so hard on him and had so adamantly warned me to stay away from him?*

Sorting through her laundry that evening, she felt the lump in the pocket of her jeans. In all the excitement, she had forgotten about the ring she'd found the day before. She studied it now. It appeared to be a woman's engagement ring, rather small in size, and hung on a cheap, old-fashioned chain. She took it downstairs to the bathroom to clean off the soot. As she started back up the hallway still examining the ring, she bumped into Raymond. "What have you got there?"

She held it up for him to see. "I found this when I went to see what was left of the house. Was it Lucille's?"

He examined her find. "No, I've never seen it before. Where exactly did you find it?"

"In the ashes around the kitchen area."

"So many people have been through there in the past few days, it could be anyone's. One of the firemen or investigators or even one of the workmen could have dropped it, I guess."

"Maybe. But it was kind of buried in the ashes." She looked troubled.

He smiled at her concern. "Well, Sherlock, like I said, there have been a lot of people roaming about. It could have been kicked around until it got buried. I wouldn't take it too seriously. I doubt if it means anything."

"So what should I do with it?"

"Hang on to it. If anyone mentions losing it, then you can return it to them. In a town this small, if it's important to someone, we'll hear about it."

She continued down the hallway and up to her room and placed the ring and chain into one of the bureau drawers for safekeeping.

There was a knock on the door, and she heard Raymond answer it.

"Rachel, there's a package for you," he called to her from the bottom of the stairs.

She walked back downstairs, retrieved the manila envelope and opened it. Inside was a new contract from Mr. Jamison for her house in Wapiti along with a note.

Dear Ms. Brittain,

I was so sorry to hear about the fire and the loss of your friend, Lucille Chavis. Mr. Warren told me that the previous contract probably burned in the fire, so I am enclosing a duplicate. Same offer. Please let me know if this is an acceptable contract. I'm anxious to close ASAP.
Sincerely,
Henry Jamison
P.S.
I hope you received the yellow rose I sent. I realized later that I had neglected to include a card.

There was no need to procrastinate any further. She wanted to stay in Eastridge with her new family, and she needed the money from the sale of the home in Wapiti. The price was more than she'd ever expected to get from the old place, so she immediately located a pen and signed the contract, feeling instant relief. It was like closing the door on a life she never wanted to revisit. She was a different person now, with an entirely new life.

Driving home the next day from a busy day of modeling, she passed by the Chavis' property. She slowed down noticing someone walking through the ruins with a metal detector. She pulled to the side of the road and parked, then recognized Nathan when he looked up to see who had arrived. She rolled her window down as he approached.

"What are you doing?"

"I lost something recently and thought I may have lost it the night of the fire."

"What was it?" She thought about the ring.

"It was something of my mother's that I've had since she's been gone. It means a lot to me. I just can't believe I lost it."

"You still haven't said what it was."

"Oh, yeah. It was a diamond ring. I wore it on a chain around my neck. Sort of my way of keeping a part of my mother with me." He looked a little embarrassed by the sentiment.

"I've got it."

He looked startled. "You've got it?"

"Yeah. I found it the day before yesterday when I was here with Collin."

"With Collin?"

"Well, actually I was here alone when Collin showed up. But the ring caught my attention when the sun reflected off it. I thought it might have been Lucille's, so I took it back to my father. But he said he'd never seen it before, so I just stuck it in my drawer until I could find out who it belonged to."

He looked relieved and bent down, grabbing her face between his hands, and kissed her on the forehead. "Thank you." He beamed.

CHAPTER 12

Monday, June 25

The courtroom swarmed with spectators and reporters with cameras flashing and bright lights from the film crews. This was the biggest headline this city had seen in decades, and everyone was engrossed. Since he'd been released from jail two weeks ago, Collin had made himself scarce. Some of the towns-people were betting that he wouldn't show up for the trial, that he would actually skip bail.

Rachel glanced at her watch. 8:55. They had been told to be there at 9:00. She turned in time to see Collin amble into the courtroom, looking totally defeated. The bailiffs were busy escorting all the news media from the room, explaining that the judge was not allowing any cameras in his courtroom.

A woman entered the courtroom with a briefcase. In her mid-thirties, short brown hair, and wearing a black pantsuit with a gray shirt, she appeared very understated and professional. She walked to the table on the front left side of the room, never acknowledging anyone. Collin sat at an adjacent table to the right with his attorney.

The bailiff announced for everyone to stand as the honorable Judge Edward Carlisle entered the room from a doorway behind the bench.

In such a small city, there were slim pickings for a jury pool. It took only a couple of hours for the attorneys to question the possible jurors and pick twelve men and women they felt would best represent Collin's peers.

After a short recess, Rachel studied the twelve that had been chosen. The first was a gray-haired gentleman, small and frail. The second was a virtuous-looking woman with long brown hair who looked to be about thirty-five. Next was an older woman with big hair and long, colorful nails. A large, balding man with glasses was seated beside her. It was an extremely diverse group. Five men, seven women. Eight white, three black, and one Asian. They ranged from twenty-five to seventy years old.

Rachel had never been in a courtroom before. The proceedings were a bit less stately than she'd expected. The judge looked bored with the formalities and mumbled through them. Then, as the attorneys began the questioning, he sat back and almost looked as if he were napping.

The prosecuting attorney, Ms. Avery, called Nathaniel Hamilton to the stand first. Nathan entered through the double doors at the rear of the room, walked briskly to the witness box and was sworn in.

"Please state your name and occupation."

"Nathaniel Hamilton, contractor."

"Mr. Hamilton, how long have you known the defendant, Collin Chavis?"

"Since he was born."

"And just how close were you to him and his family?"

"They were like a second family to me, especially after my mother left us. I stayed at their house more than I stayed at my own."

"And how would you describe Collin?"

"Well, I guess you might call him free-spirited. He was always getting into mischief as a kid. But, basically, it was all harmless stuff. He's really a pretty great guy."

"Yes, Mr. Hamilton. I realize you have some loyalties to him and his family, but please stick to the facts. The fact is that he was a trouble-maker, is that so?"

"Objection! Leading the witness." The defense attorney came alive.

Before the judge could rule, Ms. Avery agreed to re-word her question. "Was the defendant one to get into trouble a lot?"

Nathan smiled. "I can't remember a time when he wasn't in some kind of trouble with his parents. But he never did anything illegal."

"Did you see him the night of the fire?"

Nathan took in a deep breath. "Yes."

"Tell us about that evening."

"I had just come home from a dinner with Rachel, and Collin was there waiting for me."

Ms. Avery interrupted by holding up her hand. "Rachel?"

"Yes, Rachel Brittain. She was staying with the Chavises, and we've dated a couple of times."

"Okay, go on."

"Well, like I said, he was there waiting for me when I got home and was angry with me for going out with Rachel. He'd been drinking, I could tell. He was depressed and angry. He started to threaten me, saying I had better stay away from Rachel. But then he just started whining about how rotten his life was. I got him to sit down and have some coffee with me and just let him talk everything out. He started telling me how he felt about Rachel, even though she is his half sister, and then he started talking about his resentment of his brother, Justin, and how his parents adored him. And how they hated Collin and probably wished he'd never been born. The more he talked, the more angry he became, until he finally ran out of my house saying how he would show everybody."

Collin jumped out of his seat. "You're lying! I never said anything like that!"

The courtroom came alive as everyone began to talk, and the bailiff and his attorney tried to calm Collin down. The judge was banging with his gavel trying to gain control.

Finally, everything calmed down, and they continued.

"Mr. Hamilton. You were sworn to tell the truth. Are you telling the truth as you remember it?"

"Yes." He looked at Collin, his eyes full of remorse. "I'm sorry, Collin, but I had to tell the truth."

Collin's face was red, and his jaw was clenched, as were his fists as he gave Nathan a menacing stare.

"After the night of the fire, did you see the defendant?"

"No."

"How about at his mother's funeral? Surely he was there!"

"No, I didn't see him there."

"No more questions at this time."

The judge turned to the defense table, still seemingly bored. "Mr. Cabell?"

The thin, nervous man that had been hired to defend Collin stood. "Mr. Hamilton. Would you say that you and Collin were ever friends?"

"Sure, I guess so. I was closer friends with his brother, but Collin and I have always gotten along."

"Let's go back to the night of the fire. When you arrived home from your date with Miss Brittain, you said Collin was waiting for you?"

"That's right."

"And you said you could tell he had been drinking."

"Yes."

"How could you tell that? Did you give him a breath test?" His inference was that the idea that anyone could tell without a breath test was laughable.

"No, but it was pretty obvious he was drunk."

"Or maybe just upset?"

"Both drunk and upset."

"I see. So you allowed this drunk, threatening, angry person into your home for some coffee. Do you normally socialize with such people in your home?"

"I was hoping I could calm him down and help him with his problems. He's almost like a brother to me."

"Okay, now after he left, what made you go to the Chavis' home?"

"I thought about what he'd said about how he was going to show them all, and I got worried. The more I thought about his state of mind, the more concerned I became. So I drove over to their house just to be sure everything was okay."

"So that's when you saw the flames?"

"That's right."

Rachel couldn't help noticing that his testimony was almost word-for-word the same as he had told her at the restaurant, only he seemed a lot more sure now of Collin's inebriated condition.

"When you rescued Miss Brittain, which part of the house did you go through?"

"I entered the front door and went up the stairs and through Collin's room, which is the front bedroom on the left side of the house. Then out to the balcony, where I found Rachel, and back through the same way I had come."

"And did you go back in for the others after that?"

"I tried, but the flames had become too hot and thick. I couldn't get past the dining and living rooms."

The attorney turned toward the judge. "No more questions at this time, Your Honor, but I reserve the right to recall this witness at a later time."

The other witnesses for the prosecution included the investigator for the insurance company, the sheriff's office detective, and the arresting officer, 'Officer Rudie'. The insurance investigator and the detective both testified to the fact that there was absolutely no doubt it had been arson and that the fire had started in the kitchen by a flammable liquid being poured on the floor and ignited.

The detective then told how they had located an empty gasoline can behind the steel mill where Collin works and that it had Collin's fingerprints on it. One of the employees had told him that the container had not been there the day before the fire.

Officer Rudie simply testified about where and how he had arrested the defendant and how Collin had just finished 'revisiting the scene of the crime'.

After that, there were a couple of towns-people that testified that Collin had been a troubled child and how his mother had made the remark on several occasions that he would never amount to anything. They told of boyhood pranks and how none of his neighbors trusted him.

By the end of the week, it wasn't looking very favorable for the defense, but the defense attorney still had his turn coming. Rachel found herself hoping that he could come up with some kind of proof that Collin hadn't committed this crime. She hoped with all her heart that it had been a stranger that had done this horrible thing.

The entire family gathered around Aunt Marty's living room with Collin and his attorney to try to organize a good defense strategy. The television was on, but the volume was turned down as they all sat around trying to brainstorm. It seemed totally fruitless. They all believed Collin was innocent, but no one could come up with adequate proof. His only alibi was Nathan, and Nathan's testimony had all but convicted him already.

"I believe our only hope is for you to testify on your own behalf and hope the jury will see the sincerity in you. Collin, you've got to be sure that they see nothing but pure innocence. No anger or hostility. If you can show them genuine sorrow over your mother's death, that might help. They need to see your love for your family so they will know you could never do such a thing."

Collin shook his head. "It's no use. These people know of my reputation as a rebellious kid. They want to believe I'm guilty. No matter what I do or say, they will find me guilty."

Rachel ached for him. She absent-mindedly glanced toward the television just in time to see her own face staring back at her. "What are they talking about now?" She leaped across the room and turned up the volume.

The reporter was broadcasting another fabricated story, trying to top the sensational headlines being passed off as news everywhere else. The news media made even the false accounts seem like genuine news. Nothing they were saying about the Chavis's was even remotely close to the truth. Rachel would not even have recognized the stories were about her family if they weren't showing their pictures. Their faces were plastered on the front of all the newspapers, on every news broadcast, and even on all the tabloid shows. The talk shows had guests that were claiming to be neighbors or close friends of the Chavis's, yet none of the family members had ever seen them before.

This reporter was telling about how Collin, the murderer of his mother, Lucille Chavis, had been having an incestuous relationship with his sister just prior to setting the fatal fire. It was being reported that he and his brother, Justin, had been abused by their parents as young children, and it was suspected that he would use this as his defense. They had even gone as far as to suggest that Justin had left town and moved as far away as possible to escape the abuse.

Rachel couldn't believe the horrible lies. Tears streamed down her cheeks as Aunt Marty turned off the television. "Where on earth do they get that stuff? They are making this into some X-rated movie."

Mr. Cabell looked at Rachel, then glanced around the room at everyone else. "The media is making a circus out of this, but we have to try to ignore it and concentrate on proving that Collin did not set that fire. So let's try to sit down and come up with some way to prove to the rest of the world how ridiculous those stories are. I want Rachel and Mayor Shaw to testify. Hopefully, being the respected Mayor of this city will carry some weight. And Rachel can win over the jury with her innocence and purity. It will be very important that you do not lose your temper or say anything in anger. Rachel, you will have to be so above reproach and genuine that no one will possibly be able to believe the trash on that TV. And you will have to convince the jury that you believe, without any doubt, that Collin could never do such a thing."

Rachel nodded. "That's no problem. I can do that."

Then Mr. Cabell turned to Collin. "But the main witness will have to be Collin. He's the only one that knows where he was and what he was doing that night. And he will have to convince that jury that he's telling the truth."

Collin had been looking at Rachel, grateful for her confidence in him. "I'll do my best. I'm just so thankful that you all believe me. I don't know what I would do if you believed I set that fire." His eyes glistened. He quickly blinked and ducked his head, rubbing his hands across his face to hide his tears.

But Rachel had noticed and wanted desperately to reach out and comfort him.

After the attorney had left, Collin walked outside into the bright sunshine and sat by the creek, tossing pebbles into the stream. Rachel wandered over and sat next to him. They sat quietly watching the water trickle over the rocks and listening to the birds twitter. She wanted to comfort him, but was at a loss for words. Nothing she could say could change what he had to go through.

"You look deep in thought." She realized how lame it sounded, but had no idea what else to say.

"I was just noticing the stones in the creek. It's really incredible how such destructive forces like wind and water can create such beautiful stones."

They sat quietly, each lost in their own thoughts, until she couldn't suppress her questions any longer.

"Collin, tell me about the night of the fire. Where did you go when you left Nathan's?"

He continued staring into the water. "I don't want to talk about that night. I'm going to have to relive it all once this week, isn't that enough?"

"I guess you're right. I'm sorry."

An incredulous look was on his face as he turned to look at her. "You don't believe me, do you? You really think I set the fire!"

"No! I do believe you. I just wondered where you might have gone, that's all. I know you couldn't have done such a thing."

"And how would you know that? You've only known me for a couple of months."

"True. But I can't believe I'm such a bad judge of character that I could be wrong about you."

"You don't know anything about me." He stood up and angrily threw a handful of rocks into the water, then stomped off toward the house.

She watched as he disappeared into the house. All she'd wanted was to try to make him feel better and show him her support, but he wasn't making it easy for her to believe in him. He almost seemed angry with her.

She recalled her mother saying that men never know what they want or need. They are the most needy creatures on earth, she would say, but they would never admit they needed anything or anyone.

Rachel shook her head and determined that the last thing she needed was to baby-sit a man. If Collin didn't want her moral support, then she wasn't going to force it on him.

Nathan had been busy with the demolition of the old house and preparing the drawings and getting the permits for the new one, so he hadn't been around much. However, as she was walking toward the house, he drove up.

Rachel waved. "Hello there, stranger."

He smiled as he climbed out of his pick-up truck with several papers in his hand. "Hi yourself, beautiful. I've really missed you and that cheerful smile of yours."

"Well, obviously not enough or you would have called."

"Touché! I've just been really busy trying to get that house rebuilt so you can have a home again. It's all been for you, you know. I think about you constantly, and I knew the best gift I could give you would be to get the house built as quickly as possible." His mischievous grin made her giggle with delight.

"Well, sir, aren't you chivalrous. So you came here today to see me?"

"Of course."

"So are those papers for me?"

"Uh, no, actually they are for Mr. Chavis. But it is good news for you, too. I have finally received the building permit and can begin working on the new house Monday."

"Great! I love this place, but it is a little small for all of us. And I'm sure Aunt Marty will be glad to have her home to herself again. How long will it take to rebuild?"

"Depending on the weather, I think I can be finished in about four or five months."

They went into the house and were greeted by Aunt Marty and Raymond. They sat around the kitchen table and spread the house plans in front of them.

"I've already nailed the building permit up at the property and staked off the house. I just want to be sure there are no changes you want to make before I start on Monday."

"No, no changes. I want it built exactly like it was. Lucille loved that house, and we were so happy there. I want it built back exactly the same in her memory."

Rachel smiled with delight. She was so proud that her father would do such a lovely thing for the woman he'd loved. She remembered the flowers he had ordered for her mother's grave and realized what a thoughtful man he was. The circumstances of her birth and her mother's life of loneliness, she realized now, weren't caused by an inconsiderate low-life, as she'd grown up believing. They had all paid for an unfortunate mistake that anyone could have made.

That night in the solitude of her bed, she thought about her mother, her father, and Lucille, and felt confused. She no longer knew how to feel about things. All her life she'd felt anger and contempt, not only for her father, but for all men. Now suddenly she was seeing everything in an entirely new light. The anger and hostility toward men had been such a large part of who she was inside that now that it was gone, she felt numb and empty. The revelation she was experiencing should have given her a sense of relief, but instead it frightened her. All of a sudden she had no idea who she was suppose to be, or how she was suppose to feel.

She reached over and clicked on the bedside lamp and reached for her mother's Bible. It had been a long time since she'd read it, but she now felt it was the only way she could sort out her emotions. She opened the book to the book of Galatians, where a marker had been placed, and read the words her mother had underlined in red ink:

'The fruit of the Spirit is love, joy, peace, longsuffering, gentleness, goodness, faith, meekness, temperance: against such there is no law....
If we live in the Spirit, let us also walk in the Spirit.
Let us not be desirous of vain glory, provoking one another, envying one another.'

Tears ran down her cheeks as she remembered her mother. She'd been a remarkable woman, and this scripture expressed her philosophy of life. Rachel was overwhelmed by a feeling that her mother was with her and was trying to show her the way.

CHAPTER 13

Monday, July 2

Rachel couldn't believe the number of people that crowded the courthouse to hear Collin's defense. It was as much a social event for the town than anything else. Everyone was anxious to see how this 'murder trial' would end.

Collin sat next to his attorney, more nervous than ever. He was certain that no one would ever believe his side of the story. Aunt Marty was his first character witness. But he knew that, although the people of this town respected her, they also knew he was her nephew and that she would always be loyal to her family, no matter what. Therefore, her testimony probably wouldn't mean a whole lot.

Mr. Cabell asked her a few simple questions about Collin's integrity, then offered Ms. Avery, the prosecutor, her turn.

After Aunt Marty had testified, it was Rachel's turn. She'd been tense all morning, but now that the time had come, she found that she was calm and determined to get her point across. The defense attorney stood waiting as she was sworn in, then approached her with a tender smile, attempting to make her feel comfortable and at ease. "Miss Brittain, can you tell the court what your relationship is with the Chavis's?"

"Yes. Raymond Chavis is my father."

"And you are residing with your father?"

"Yes."

"So would you say you know Collin Chavis pretty well since you live under the same roof?"

"Yes."

"Were you at home the night of the fire?"

"Yes."

"Tell us what you remember about that night."

"Well, I was asleep and thought I was dreaming when I started choking from the smoke. It was dark, and I tried to run to the door, but it was so hot, and the smoke was so thick I couldn't breath. So I crawled along the floor to the balcony door."

"Do you know if Collin was at home?"

"I thought he was, so I went to his balcony door and banged on it, screaming for him. But he didn't answer."

"So then what happened?"

"Someone grabbed me from behind and wrapped me in a wet blanket and carried me down the stairs and out the front door."

"Do you know who it was that rescued you?"

"Yes, it was Nathan Hamilton."

"Nathan Hamilton?" Mr. Cabell turned and looked into the courtroom and looked straight into Nathan's eyes. Then he turned back to Rachel, looking confused. "Now how did Nathan Hamilton just happen to be there?"

"He's a good friend of the family. He comes over quite often." She wasn't sure what the attorney was trying to get at, but she didn't want to bring up the fact that Nathan had been worried about what Collin might do.

"I see." He looked suspiciously back at Nathan. "Okay, let's move on. Do you believe that Collin is capable of burning down his family's home and killing his mother?"

"No." She was adamant. "He loved his mother and father. There is no way he would ever do anything that might hurt them or me."

"Your witness, Counselor." He sat at the defense table and scribbled a few notes as the prosecutor stood and approached Rachel, grinning slyly.

"Miss Brittain? is it?"

"That's right."

"How is it that you are Raymond Chavis's daughter but have the last name of Brittain? Are you married?"

Mr. Cabell jumped to his feet. "Objection! Irrelevant."

"Sustained." The judge looked bored.

Ms. Avery still looked smug. "Okay, *MISS* Brittain, how long have you lived with the Chavis family?"

"Since the middle of April."

"This year?"

"Yes."

"Gee, that's only about two months."

"That's right."

"How well did you know them prior to that time?"

"I didn't."

"What do you mean?"

"I did not know the Chavis's at all until I met them in April."

"So you didn't know your father or his family while you were a child."

"No."

"So you really don't know Collin very well at all, do you?"

"I feel like I do."

"But at the time of the fire, you had only known him for a few short weeks. Is that correct?"

"A little over a month, actually."

"So in reality, Collin was—no, correction—Collin IS a virtual stranger to you." Before Rachel could respond, Ms. Avery quickly looked at the judge and uttered "No more questions."

Rachel was excused from the witness chair and felt she had failed at helping Collin's case.

Collin's attorney was looking nervous and worried. His only hope was that Collin could convince the jury of his innocence. He had absolutely nothing else tangible to prove it could be someone else. If he could just come up with a motive for someone else, but so far he had nothing. "We now call the defendant, Collin Chavis, to the stand."

Collin took a deep breath, glanced at the jurors, and walked confidently to the witness box and was sworn in.

Mr. Cabell addressed him firmly. "Please state your name."

"Collin Chavis."

"Mr. Chavis, Nathaniel Hamilton claimed in his testimony that you were at his home the night of the fire. Could you tell us about that visit."

"Yes. I did go to his house that night to tell him to stay away from Rachel."

"Had you been drinking?"

"No."

"Were you angry?"

"Not really angry, just upset."

"So you had not been drinking and you were not angry?"

"That's right."

"So what did happen when you got there?"

"I told Nathan that I wanted him to stay away from Rachel. He seemed to understand how I felt and asked me to come in and talk about it. He offered me a few drinks, and we talked."

"Mr. Hamilton testified that he offered you coffee to help get you sober."

"He never offered any coffee. I hadn't had anything alcoholic to drink until he mixed us a few drinks."

"Okay, so what happened next?"

Collin looked down and closed his eyes for a second, realizing how lame his next admission would sound. "I passed out on his sofa."

"So you slept there all night?"

"I don't really know what happened. The next thing I knew I was waking up in my car behind the steel mill. I don't know how I got there. I don't remember anything else."

"What time was it when you did wake up?"

"Late, but I don't know the exact time. I believe it was after midnight, but I never looked at a clock."

This was not looking good for his client. The best he could hope for at this point was guilty by reason of insanity, or drunken stupor. The jurors wouldn't be too willing to accept this scenario. He decided to change his line of questioning.

"Collin, no one saw you for quite a few hours after the fire. Why is that?"

"I had a terrible hangover when I woke up in my car and didn't want to face anybody. I was so upset that I just wanted to get away and think things through."

"What were you so upset about? Did you know about the fire?"

"No. I had no idea about any of that. I was upset about learning that Rachel was my half sister. I was in love with her, and to find out that my father was her father was unbearable. I felt ashamed and sick. I just wanted to run away from it all."

"So where did you go?"

"Turtle Creek. I stayed the rest of the night and the next day there and drove back home on Monday morning."

"When did you learn about the fire?"

"When I got home I saw the house had burned down. I didn't know what to think. I didn't know if anyone had survived." His eyes watered, and a tear slipped down his cheek. "I banged on the neighbor's door and was told to go to the hospital. So I did, and that's when they told me my mother had died." He looked down, not wanting everyone to witness his tears.

Mr. Cabell asked the bailiff for a glass of water and gave Collin a chance to collect himself.

"No one saw you for several days after your mother passed away. In fact, some say you didn't even go to the funeral. Can you explain this disappearance?"

"I did go to the funeral, but I just didn't feel up to everyone's pity and fake pleasantries. I just wanted to avoid all of that and try to handle my own grief. I wandered around for several days, mostly at Turtle Creek. When I finally pulled myself together enough to come back and face the pain, they arrested me."

"Collin, did you set the fire to your family's home?"

"No. I loved my family and that house. It was my home. I could never have done such a thing. Almost everyone I cared about in the entire world was in that house at the time of the fire. Why would I want to do that?" He could contain himself no longer and began to weep uncontrollably. "I loved my mother."

There wasn't a dry eye in the courtroom, except the judge and the prosecutor. However, even Judge Carlisle didn't look bored any more.

The prosecutor stood and applauded slowly. "Very good performance, Mr. Chavis. Let me see if I understand this story you have so skillfully laid out for us."

"Objection, Your Honor."

"Sustained. Ms. Avery, please do away with the theatrics."

"Sorry, Your Honor." She walked slowly toward Collin, seemingly in deep thought. "Okay, Mr. Chavis. You would have us to believe that you went to Mr. Hamilton's home and fell asleep on the sofa. Then you don't remember anything else until you woke up in your car."

"That's right."

"And where was your car parked?"

"Behind the steel mill."

She smiled and shook her head. "You know, that's quite a coincidence. That is exactly where the sheriff's office found the empty gasoline can that hadn't been there the day before. How do you explain that?"

"I don't know anything about any gas can. I woke up there, and then I drove to Turtle Creek."

"Why would you go to Turtle Creek? Were you trying to hide?"

"No, I just wanted to get away. I explained that already."

"Oh, yes. You were upset. But why Turtle Creek?"

"I used to go there a lot. I don't know why I picked there. I just drove, and that's where I wound up."

"Did anyone see you there?"

"Yes. I stayed with an old friend."

"So we could verify that you were there and at what time?"

"Well, yes. But I'd rather keep them out of it."

"Oh? You're facing a murder charge, but you don't want your only alibi involved?"

"I didn't do it! And I don't want to cause trouble for anyone else."

"Anyone else? You mean like the trouble you caused your family when you set that fire?"

"No. I didn't set any fire."

"And how would you know that if you don't even remember driving to the steel mill? You are expecting us to believe that you can't remember leaving Nathaniel Hamilton's house. So according to your own story, you can't even know if you burned your house down or not."

"I wouldn't have done that."

"But you *don't remember*."

Collin looked at his attorney for help, but he could see the hopelessness displayed on Mr. Cabell's face. He knew he was going to prison, and there was nothing he could do about it.

Ms. Avery was far from finished with him. "Mr. Chavis, is it true that you and your parents didn't get along?"

"We got along. We had disagreements just like all kids and their parents."

"No, not like all kids. You had just learned that your father had cheated on your mother. Weren't you angry at him for that?"

"Sure. I couldn't believe he would do such a thing. Any kid would feel betrayed by that."

"And because of his betrayal, now you were learning that the woman you loved was actually your half-sister. Is that right?"

"Yes."

"That would make most people a little crazy."

"Not crazy, just troubled."

"Troubled? I don't believe that could begin to describe what you must have felt."

"I don't know how else to describe it. I was hurt and confused."

"Sometimes when people are hurt, they lash out."

"But I didn't. Not the way you mean."

"Witnesses have told us how your mother was always saying you wouldn't amount to anything. And you've told us how 'hurt and confused' you were by what your father had done. And Rachel was seeing your friend Nathan, and that made you angry, didn't it?"

"No. I didn't like it, but I wasn't angry."

"So, these three people who had so disappointed you were in the house, and what better way to teach them a lesson but to burn the house down with all of them in it. Isn't that how it happened?"

Collin jumped up out of his seat. "NO! I didn't do it. I loved my mother and Rachel. I could never have hurt them."

"But, you don't remember," she added sarcastically. "No more questions." She had made her point. Now it was time to shut up and let it all sink into the jurors' minds.

Court was adjourned for the day, to be continued the next morning at 9:00 AM.

CHAPTER 14

Tuesday, July 3

It was 8:45 AM. Collin sat at the defense table, his head in his hands, knowing that his case was weak. He had nothing to offer that could help his situation, so he was resigned to going to prison for a long time.

Rachel slid into the courtroom and observed his aura of hopelessness. Concerned, she approached him timidly, tapping him on his shoulder. "Collin, I just wanted to let you know I'm here for you."

He glanced up at her, the despair so clearly portrayed in his tired eyes. She ached for someone to prove he didn't commit this horrendous deed. Now that they knew they were not brother and sister, would they get the chance to experience those feelings that had been so powerful?

Court was called to order. She took her seat, her mind suddenly jolted back to the reality of the moment. More and more it was appearing that Collin was guilty. And if that were the case, she could never feel anything for him but contempt.

"Mr. Cabell, do you have any other witnesses?" It seemed that the judge just wanted this case to hurry up and be over.

"Yes, Your Honor. The defense calls Melissa Evans to the stand."

Collin stood up and grabbed his attorney's arm. "What are you doing? I told you I didn't want her involved."

The judge banged his gavel. "Mr. Cabell, please get control of your client."

"I'm sorry, Your Honor, please give us a moment to confer."

Collin and the attorney sat down and whispered back and forth heatedly for a few minutes.

"What is the problem, Mr. Cabell?" Judge Carlisle was becoming impatient.

"My client thought I had summoned Ms. Evans to be here, but the fact is that she came forward on her own, wanting to testify."

"Mr. Chavis, are we ready to resume?"

"Do I have a choice?"

"No, but if there are any more outbursts in my court, I will hold you in contempt. Is that clear?"

"Yes sir."

"Bailiff, send in the witness."

Melissa Evans walked through the double doors and glanced around the courtroom as she approached the witness stand. She was a blond petite girl that had once been a beauty, but it was apparent that she had lived a hard life. Her eyes were weak and sad with dark bags beneath them, her hair hung limp, and there were bruises and scars on her legs and arms. She gave Collin a half-hearted smile as she sat in the witness chair after being sworn in.

"Please state your name for the court."

"Melissa Ross Evans."

"Ms. Evans, where do you live?"

"Turtle Creek."

"And do you know the defendant, Collin Chavis?"

"Yes, we have been friends for a long time."

"Do you remember where you were the night of June 2nd?"

"Yes, I was at home."

"And did you see anyone that night?"

"Yes, Collin came to see me."

"Do you know what time he arrived?"

"I believe it was about one, or one-thirty, in the morning."

"How far is Turtle Creek from here?"

"I don't know exactly how many miles, but it takes about an hour to drive there."

"So to get to your house by one o'clock, he would have to leave here by midnight. Correct?"

"Yeah, that's right."

"And what time did he leave your house?"

"He didn't leave until about seven on Monday morning."

"And you were with him the entire time?"

"Yes, every minute."

"Thank you Ms. Evans. No more questions."

"Ms. Avery?" The judge took a deep breath as he doggedly pushed the proceedings along.

"Thank you, Your Honor." She approached with an air of confidence and a sneer. "Ms. Evans. Now is that a Miss or a Mrs.?"

"I'm going through a divorce. I'm legally separated."

"I see...so you just decided to fill the empty nights with another man?"

"Objection! Ms. Evans's private life is of no concern here, Your Honor."

Ms. Avery looked at Mr. Cabell as if he were very stupid indeed. "I disagree. Mrs. Evans is a very important witness, and her credibility is very pertinent to this case."

The judge shrugged. "I'll allow it, but be careful where you go with this line of questioning."

"Of course. Mrs. Evans, how can you be so sure that it was June 2nd that Collin showed up at your door?"

"Because Sunday, June 3, was my daughter's birthday, and Collin helped us celebrate it."

"So you have a daughter? How nice. How old is she?"

"She's two."

"And is your husband her father?"

"My ex-husband. Yes." She glanced at Collin, looking slightly uneasy.

"He's not your ex yet, Mrs. Evans. But where was he on his daughter's birthday?"

"He couldn't be there because I have a restraining order against him."

Ms. Avery decided to change her line of questioning. The last thing she wanted was for the jury to pity this witness.

"When Mr. Chavis arrived at your home, what kind of mood was he in?"

"He was confused and upset."

"And did he tell you why he was upset?"

"Yes, he'd been to talk to Nathan Hamilton and fell asleep on his couch. When he woke up, he was in his car at the steel mill. He couldn't understand how he got there."

"Well, I admit, that is strange." She looked at the jury and rolled her eyes as if she didn't believe a word of it.

"Is that all that he was upset about?"

"No. He was also upset that Nathan was making moves on Rachel and that he'd just learned recently that Rachel was his half-sister."

"Was he drunk when he came to your house?"

"No."

"Okay. So Collin was upset and came to you for comfort. What kind of relationship do you have?"

"What do you mean? We're friends."

"I mean, are you lovers?"

"No, not really."

"So you didn't sleep together that entire week-end?"

Melissa ducked her head and mumbled, "Yes."

"Please speak up so we can hear you."

She looked up and at Collin. "Yes, we slept together. But we were just both terribly unhappy and tried to make each other forget our problems. That's all."

"So do you always sleep with other guys just to forget your problems?"

"No, not always." She glared at the attorney. "You gonna tell me that you've never slept around, Miss Perfect?"

Mr. Cabell had heard enough. "Your Honor, could the prosecution make her point. This is ridiculous."

"I agree," the judge looked pointedly at Ms. Avery. "Let's get on with it, Counselor."

"Mrs. Evans, do you love Collin Chavis?"

Melissa looked at Collin and then down at her hands in her lap. "Yes."

"And you would do anything for him, wouldn't you?" Ms. Avery was being gentle suddenly.

"Yes."

Now it was time to drive her point home, her fake sensitivity turning into a wicked smugness. "The fact is you love him so much that you were willing to come here today and say anything that you thought would help him stay out of jail. Isn't that right?"

Melissa was still thinking about her admission that she loved Collin, and the attorney's attack had taken her by surprise. "Yes. I mean, no. I..."

"No more questions."

The defense was doomed, and they all knew it. Mr. Cabell didn't have anything else to present.

Rachel sat looking at the once-pretty blond that was leaving the witness chair. Then she looked at Collin. She'd wanted so badly to believe in his innocence, but she could no longer continue to ignore the facts.

Collin urged his attorney to put him back on the stand so he could have one last chance to make an impression on the jury before they went to decide his fate and, realizing the case was all but lost anyway, he agreed.

Mr. Cabell stood back and asked only one question. "Collin, is there anything you would like to say on your own behalf at this time?"

He sat looking very humble and sincere. "Your Honor and members of the jury, I just want to assure you that I could not, and would not ever hurt my mother or anyone else in my family." He looked at his rooting section, and tears overflowed onto his cheeks as he turned back to the jurors. "I may not have shown them, but I love each and every one of them. Especially my mother. She was my strength and the only one that I felt really knew me.

Sure we had disagreements, the way all kids do with their parents. I don't know what happened that night because, as I've told you, I passed out and then woke back up at the steel mill. I don't remember anything in between those two periods of time. I wish I did. I do know that if you'll give me the chance, I will never touch alcohol again, and I will make my mother proud of me somehow. I want to be able to show my family how much I love them, and I want to find out what really happened that night so I can prove to you, and to myself, that I had nothing to do with it. Please give me the opportunity to do that, I beg you." He was sobbing uncontrollably as he left the witness stand.

Rachel looked at the jurors. Some of them looked moved by his emotional speech, but others had faces of stone, showing no sign of compassion at all. She looked back at Collin, his head resting on his hands on the table and his shoulders still quaking from his crying.

She wondered. Was this a grand act to win the sympathy of the jury? If so, it had been an Emmy-winning performance. She thought back to the Collin she had first met. That impish and taunting smile that she'd hated so at first, but had learned to love, was gone now. It had been replaced by a look of desperation and pain. She was so confused. She wanted to believe in him. But after talking with Nathan and listening closely to the prosecutor's closing statement, even she was convinced that he had set the fire. Maybe he hadn't known what he was doing at the time, but it had caused Lucille's death, and someone had to pay for that.

Rachel nervously walked the courthouse hallway along with the rest of the family. "Aunt Marty, what kind of sentence is he facing if they find him guilty?"

The older woman stared down at the floor and spoke as if talking to herself. "First, they have to decide if he is guilty of the arson. According to the 'felony murder law', if you set a fire and someone dies, you are automatically guilty of murder. So, worst-case scenario is a sentencing of life imprisonment for aggravated arson and murder. Usually, unless a jury believes the intent was murder, they ignore this law. All we can do is hope and pray."

The jury took four hours to deliberate. When they returned, they found Collin 'guilty' of the arson charge; 'not guilty' of murder, but rather 'guilty' of involuntary manslaughter. Sentencing was to be in one week.

CHAPTER 15

Thursday, July 5

Independence Day had come and gone. The family hadn't felt much like celebrating so they'd indulged in a quiet and relaxing day at home.

Monroe had been exceptionally understanding about her having to take time off to be with her family during the trial. But now it was over, and it was time to get back to work. She breezed into the offices and began reviewing everything that had been done while she'd been away. She had only missed one important show and needed to catch up on the preparations for the next one.

The entire town, including everyone at Milliken's, was gossiping about the trial and Collin's imprisonment. Whenever she entered a room, everything became hushed. It created a lot of tension for her, making it difficult to concentrate on anything.

By Friday, it had already become old news, and the world was back to normal, Collin totally forgotten. Even Rachel's busy schedule didn't allow her time to commiserate about his fate.

It was Saturday morning brunch, and all the renowned upper class were gathered together to view the latest Milliken fashions. The show had been publicized as 'The Event of the Season'. Rachel was proud of her performance in spite of the whispers she heard as she passed by some of the tables. She could only hope that these were comments about the clothing.

A huge success, the show produced more sales than any past presentations.

Returning to Aunt Marty's a little after 2:00 that afternoon, Rachel was totally exhausted. She'd hoped to get her swimsuit on, soak up a few rays in the back yard and take a much-needed nap, but Nathan was waiting for her when she arrived. His car was parked under a tree near the house, and he was sitting on the stoop by the front door, beaming when he saw her approaching.

He stood and waved. "Hey, it's about time you got home. I've been waiting forever to see you."

"Why, what's up?"

"I've missed you, that's all. We haven't seen each other for a while, and I hoped we could go grab a bite to eat."

She gave him her most apologetic look and shook her head. "I'm sorry, Nathan, but I've had a grueling morning and would really just like to take a nap. I'm not really hungry."

"Sure, I understand. How did the show go?"

"It went great, couldn't have been better. It just really wore me out."

He nodded with a disappointed smile. "Okay. Why don't you get some rest, and maybe you'll feel more like going out later for dinner. Can I check with you this evening?"

"Maybe a late dinner. Give me a call around six o'clock."

His spirits lifted. "Six it is," and he left.

The shrill noise of the telephone startled her as it destroyed the calmness of the afternoon. She'd been in the lounge chair for a couple of hours, dozing peacefully. She glanced at her watch--*6:00 exactly. It must be Nathan.*

"Chavis residence."

"Hey sleepy-head. It's time to eat. Hungry yet?"

"Sure, why not. Give me an hour to get myself together. I'll see you around seven, okay?"

"I'll be there."

Millstone Terrace was a plantation-style building alongside the golf course. It possessed a romantic atmosphere and was more relaxed than the country club. Rachel had heard of it, but this was her first visit.

Nathan had reserved one of the best tables with a window view of a lovely fountain and flower gardens. A bottle of wine was already chilling on the table. Beside it was a long gift box. The hostess sat her in front of the box, and Nathan beckoned her to open it. Inside were a dozen long-stem red roses, freshly cut. Before she could remove them from the box, the hostess returned with a tall crystal vase and helped arrange them for her.

"Please keep the vase with our compliments."

"Thank you."

The dinner was perfect, the evening more like a dream than reality. After eating, they took a stroll around the gardens and enjoyed a warm breeze. They found a bench, and she sat with her eyes closed, breathing the sweet fragrance of the summer air mixed with the flowers and freshly mowed grass. Nathan sat quietly watching her.

A few minutes passed before she looked at him and gave him a warm smile. "Thank you so much for tonight. It's just what I needed."

"There could be many nights like this for us. My greatest wish is for you and me to share all of our evenings for the rest of our lives."

She was startled, and slightly embarrassed, by this declaration and couldn't speak at first. She looked at him wide-eyed trying to figure out if he were truly serious. "Wh—where did that come from?"

"I'm sorry. I didn't mean to spring it on you so soon, but the setting was just so ideal. The truth is, I knew I wanted you for my wife the moment I met you. Collin saw it in my face, and that's what upset him so much."

The mention of Collin made her think of him sitting in the jail cell all alone. She felt almost guilty enjoying herself. The romantic spell had been broken. All she wanted was to go home. "I'm sorry, Nathan, but I really would like to be going now." She grabbed her handbag and started quickly toward the parking lot.

"Hold on, Cinderella, it's not midnight yet. What's your hurry?" He grabbed her elbow and tugged on it to slow her down. She stopped, but stood facing the parking lot. "Is it something I said?"

"No, of course not," and she turned and faced him with sad eyes. "I'm just rather tired. It was a beautiful evening, and I do hope we can do it again soon." She was trying to be gracious, and it was apparent to Nathan that her words were polite, but empty.

Rachel attended church services with Raymond on Sunday morning and, afterwards, accompanied him to see the new house construction. The demolition phase was complete. Little evidence of the original house remained except for the footing.

Raymond explained, "Nathan said the foundation was weakened by the extreme heat of the fire, but the footing hadn't been damaged and can be used for the new construction."

Glancing around, Rachel noticed the brick had been delivered, and there was a pile of sand for the mortar. Everything was ready for the bricklayers to begin the foundation.

She thought of Collin as they stood looking at the construction site. *What on earth could have caused him to do such a thing?* She felt like such a fool to have believed in him. Lucille had warned her about him and had been right all along. Unfortunately, being right hadn't been able to save her from him. He had killed the one person that had known him better than anyone and had loved him nonetheless.

When they arrived back at Aunt Marty's, there was a message for her from Mr. Warren in Wapiti. She returned his call. "Mr. Warren?"

"Yes, hello Rachel! I'm so glad you called me back. Mr. Jamison has received loan approval, and his attorney has set the closing on your mother's house for July 27th."

"Oh, so soon," her voice was faint. It saddened her to let go of her childhood home. It was all that was left of her past. She not only felt she was betraying her mother, but turning her back on who she really was. Also, selling the house had such finality about it. There was no turning back, no going home again.

Yet it certainly didn't make any sense to keep the old place. And the money would come in handy. She'd already discussed with her father about buying the car. It was in Lucille's name, and Raymond felt that Lucille would have wanted her to have it, but Rachel insisted on paying him for it anyway. Using her first big paycheck from her modeling, she'd made a couple of payments, but it would feel good to have it paid off.

"Rachel? Are you still there?"

"Yes, I'm here. Is there anything I need to do?"

Mr. Warren explained she would have to find an attorney to prepare the deed before they could proceed any further. She knew her father would help her with that, and she assured him that she would take care of it as quickly as possible.

The doorbell rang as she hung up the phone. When she opened the door, there was a young woman holding an exquisite bouquet of flowers.

"Are you Rachel Brittain?"

"Yes."

"Good. These are for you." She handed them to her and smiled. "Someone cares a lot." She quickly turned and walked back to her van.

The card read *'Thank you for a very special evening. All my love, Nathan'*. Relief swept over her, as well as warm tender feelings for Nathan. She had been afraid that she had ruined the evening with her moodiness at the end of the night, but he'd obviously understood and not been upset by it.

She placed the arrangement in the center of the kitchen table and dialed the phone.

"Hello," he answered half-yawning.

"Thank you for the flowers. They are gorgeous. When can I see you to thank you properly?"

Suddenly he was energized. "How about right now?"

"What if I go by the store and pick up a few things and come over there and fix you dinner?"

"Sounds like a plan!"

An hour later she was in his kitchen trying to find pots and pans and utensils. Cooking in a strange kitchen wasn't as easy as was portrayed on television. They always made it look so simple and romantic. But she learned quickly that it would take her all night if she didn't get help. She marched into the den where he was watching the news, grabbed his hand and pulled him to his feet. Then she turned him toward the kitchen and pushed him. "If we are going to eat tonight, you are going to have to help."

"But you said you were going to cook me dinner."

"Yes, I know what I said, but I can't find anything in your kitchen. You can just sit at the table if you want and watch, but I need you to tell me where everything is."

He smiled and drew her to him, "I've got a better idea. I want us to do things as a team, always. We might as well begin by fixing dinner together." He kissed her nose and turned to a cupboard, pulling out two bib-style aprons.

It was a romantic evening with candlelight and soft music and plenty of wine. Rachel, feeling warm all over, sat on the floor and leaned on the sofa, closing her eyes and swaying to the music. She had never experienced such a sensation of total relaxation. The entire outside world had ceased to exist, and nothing mattered except this moment in time. Nathan joined her on the floor and pulled her to him so that she leaned her head on his shoulder. He nuzzled at her ear and neck and played with her hair. She felt safe with him and enjoyed his arms around her. She'd never felt so relaxed...

She opened her eyes, confused. The sun was shining through the window, and she was in a strange bed.

The door opened, and Nathan entered with a glass of tomato juice and a wide-awake smile. "Good morning. I thought you could use this. It sometimes helps ease the morning-after haze."

"The morning after?"

"Yeah, you had a bit too much wine last night, I'd say."

"So what happened?" She was almost afraid to ask. Her stomach was a little queasy, but she wasn't sure how she would feel if they had slept together. Not having had the experience before, she didn't know what to expect. She certainly hoped she would at least remember her first time.

Nathan quickly grasped what she was thinking. "Don't worry, nothing happened. You simply fell asleep while I was holding you. So I picked you up and brought you up here."

She looked under the covers. She was still wearing the dress she'd worn the night before. Relief swept over her, and she smiled up at him, trying to sound like Scarlett O'Hara, "Why Mr. Hamilton, I believe you truly are a gentleman."

She needed to be at work, but first she had to get home and shower and change. She crept into the house hoping everyone would still be asleep, but Aunt Marty was in the kitchen preparing coffee and muffins.

"Rachel, is that you?" she bellowed.

"Yes, it's me."

"Good. Come on in here and have some coffee with me."

She walked to the kitchen doorway and peeked in. "I really don't have time. I need to change and get to work."

"Oh, fiddlesticks. You have to have breakfast. Now take a minute to eat a muffin anyway."

"Maybe after I shower, if I have time." She scurried down the hall before Aunt Marty could argue with her further.

Driving to work, she thought about Collin. *How could I have been so wrong about him? I was such a stupid naive fool over him. Then there's Nathan. He's so warm and caring, such a perfect gentleman. I just wish I felt that same burning desire for him that I felt when I was around Collin. Maybe I will one day.*

But Collin. She thought about him sitting in a jail cell, alone. She knew she should probably go visit him, but she couldn't bring herself to go. He was the reason Lucille was dead. She couldn't forgive him for that. And he could have just as well killed her and her father, too, if it hadn't been for Nathan.

Collin walked around the large 'activities' room trying to stay clear of the other inmates. *I'm not like them. I don't belong here. I'm not a criminal. This is all a big mistake.*

He looked up and noticed a burly guy with a scruffy beard and bad teeth staring at him. As their eyes met, the other man sneered. "Pretty boy here thinks he's better than the rest of us. He doesn't want to associate with the likes of us." A few others drifted into a semi-circle around Collin. "So, Pretty Boy, what are you in here for anyway?"

Collin scanned the room for an escape route, deciding his best bet was to look tough. "Murder."

All the others snickered and looked at each other, then burst out in a full guffaw. "Yeah, right. What did you kill, a frog?"

"My mother."

They all fell silent, scrutinizing him with evil eyes.

A giant black man with red eyes stepped forward. "A man ought to have respect for his mama, boy. You better be pulling our leg."

Suddenly Collin didn't feel so tough. His fear made him crumble. "I didn't do it, I swear. I loved my mother."

"Aw shucks, he loved his mother. Did you hear that?" They all began to laugh and taunt him. Collin looked around and saw that even the guards were enjoying the joke. He started toward the exit door, but was blocked by two of them.

The giant black man waved them back. "Let him go." He gave Collin a slight smile as he stood in front of the others to let him by.

Collin returned to his cell and sat on his bunk. His cellmates were gone, and he enjoyed one of the few moments of solitude. He wished he would hear from Rachel. His father had been to see him, and he'd received a letter from Justin. They both seemed to believe that he hadn't set the fire. And, of course, Melissa knew he hadn't done it. But he needed to know that Rachel still believed in him. She was the only one that truly mattered. He wondered if she was with Nathan. The thought drove him crazy with jealousy. Nathan was the reason he was in this horrible place. It had been his testimony that had put him here. *If only I could remember what had happened between the time I passed out at Nathan's and the time I woke up at the steel mill.* He'd heard of people who had episodes when they lost time. They wouldn't be able to remember periods of time, and during these 'black-outs', would do things that they didn't remember doing. His heart began to pound, and his eyes watered, the fear within him was suffocating. He didn't want to believe he'd done it. He just wanted to run, but there was nowhere to go. He didn't want to think anymore. His head pounding, he grabbed it with both hands and squeezed trying to stop the panic his thoughts were creating. *Rachel, where are you?*

Rachel hurried into the kitchen to grab a quick cup of coffee before heading to Milliken's and found Aunt Marty dressed and preparing coffee and danish for a quick breakfast. "Good morning, Aunt Marty. You're raring to go this morning, aren't you?"

"I just wanted to be sure we all got to the courthouse in plenty of time so we can show Collin our support."

Rachel didn't respond as she retrieved a mug from the cupboard and reached for the coffee pot.

"We should get there by eight thirty at the latest. Court starts at nine, and we need to show everyone that we believe in our boy, Collin."

Still, she did not react, but remained with her back to the older woman.

"Rachel, you are going, aren't you? You will be there?"

Slowly she turned, but could not look into Aunt Marty's pleading eyes. She shook her head, her gaze remaining toward the floor. "I need to get to work this morning."

She was startled when Aunt Marty's fist thundered down onto the wooden table. "No you don't! You are now a part of this family, and I expect you to act like it! When one of our family has his back against the wall, the rest of us rally to help. That's what families are for. Either you are a part of that or you're not. And if you're not, then I will not tolerate you calling yourself a member of this family." Her eyes blazed with passion as she awaited Rachel's reply.

Rachel was so shocked by the outburst that she froze, her eyes wide and her mouth gaping. When she realized that the other woman was finished and waiting for her decision, all she could do was nod and say weakly, "okay."

"Okay, what?"

"Okay, I'll be there."

"Good. Then sit down and have a danish." She retrieved an apple danish from the cookie sheet and handed it to her.

Collin entered the double doors of the courtroom, scanning the room for Rachel. He smiled with relief when he saw her sitting with his Aunt Marty and his father. *He may not be my biological father, but he will always be my Dad.* He had never felt so much love for his family as he did at this moment. He knew Justin couldn't be here, but he had said in his letter that he knew he was innocent, and that meant more to Collin than his physical presence. *There is nothing on this earth more important than family. You can't count on anything else.*

Again, the double doors parted, and Nathan walked in. They glared at each other. Collin believed that Nathan knew what had happened that night and had fabricated this lie so he would go to prison. He had to believe that. The only other explanation was too frightening. He watched as Nathan took a seat beside Rachel, and an empty void filled Collin's chest when Rachel smiled and took Nathan's hand.

The judge entered, and the bailiff called the court to order. It was a quick hearing, mostly a formality, before the jurors were sent out to deliberate on what they felt a fair and just punishment would be.

An hour later, the jury returned with their decision. Five years behind bars.

CHAPTER 16

Saturday, October 13

Three months later....
She could hear the muffled voices of the guests filling the church. She studied herself in the mirror, admiring the exquisite white gown and veil that her father had bought for this momentous event. Monroe had designed it expressly for her.

Aunt Marty breezed into the room electrified by the intensity of the moment. "Everyone has arrived, and the minister is ready. They will begin the music in a few minutes! We have to hurry and get you ready."

"Calm down, I'm almost ready. All I need is to add a little powder and lipstick."

"Be careful not to get any on that fabulous dress."

"It's not a dress, Aunt Marty," she giggled, "it's my wedding gown."

"Gown, dress, whatever. Just don't get any makeup on it."

The final touches were complete, and she was ready to take those slow, deliberate steps down the aisle. Aunt Marty was her maid of honor, and Milly was one of her bridesmaids. And, of course, her father was giving her away.

Natalie, the model that had been so good to her when she was learning the trade, had returned to town just to be a bridesmaid in her wedding. She had been in New York making a name for herself as one of the top models in the country. This was quite an accomplishment for a black girl from a small mid-western town. *Maybe there's hope for an Indian, too.*

She went to the window and looked at the sky. "Well, Momma, this is it. I wish you were here. At least I've got my father now, thanks to Lucille. I hope you both are looking down and smiling on me today. I love you."

She took a deep breath and turned back to Aunt Marty, who was anxiously standing by trying hard to respect her time to reflect. "Okay, let's go."

The organ volume intensified when she approached the doorway to the church sanctuary. Natalie and Milly were already making their way slowly toward the front, and Aunt Marty stood ready for her turn.

The music grew even louder, then the wedding march began. Raymond took her hand and placed it on his arm, smiling lovingly into her eyes as tears spilled over his cheeks. "My beautiful little girl. I'm so happy that I could be here for this. I never thought I would have this opportunity. I love you."

"I love you too, Dad." She kissed his cheek, and they began their slow, methodical walk toward the pulpit. Her eyes locked on a pair of old gray eyes. Mr. Jamison stood at the end of the rear pew, his peaceful and loving expression somehow calming her nerves. She didn't understand why, but there was something about that man that comforted her. Since he'd purchased her mom's house, they'd remained in touch.

Upon reaching the front of the church, her father took her hand from his arm and placed it into Nathan's hand.

"Take care of her, son."

Nathan smiled knowingly and nodded. He couldn't speak. He was utterly mesmerized by his good fortune to be marrying such a stunning woman. *Collin, eat your heart out.*

Collin sat on his bunk. He'd read the announcement in the newspaper. Rachel hadn't been to see him at all. She obviously believed everything Nathan had told her, and now she was marrying that son-of-a-bitch.

Three months of being locked up, knowing he would never be able to convince Rachel of his innocence, had zapped him of any will to live. He'd lost over ten pounds and hadn't shaved in weeks. His eyes were dark and impassive, mirroring his soul.

The plane trip had been a long one, but they'd finally arrived. The cab scurried through the winding roads. Rachel was fascinated by the unspoiled beauty that surrounded her. Austria was the most extraordinary place she'd ever seen or imagined. It was just like a picture book with its white-capped mountains and glorious blue sky. The villages in the valleys were so charming.

"How much further to the ski resort?" Nathan was tired and anxious.

"Not far. Just little bit more." The driver's English was broken, but at least he could communicate reasonably well.

Nathan directed his attention to Rachel. "Justin wanted to meet us at the airport, but with his wife being about ready to deliver, he was afraid to leave her."

"When you wouldn't tell me where we were going, I was a bit uneasy.

But you couldn't have planned a more wonderful surprise. Not only is this the most fabulous place I've ever seen, but I'll be able to get to know my brother. Thank you." Her eyes twinkled with excitement and affection for her new husband. He just hoped he could always keep her as happy as she appeared to be at this moment. That was his greatest desire.

The cab finally approached the resort. Signs pointed the way to the clubhouse, the restaurant, the cabins, and the lifts. At last one of them read 'registration', and above it was 'sich eintragen' with an arrow that pointed the way for them.

Rachel sat warming herself by the fireplace in the expansive social room of the lodge, admiring her older half-brother. "You are so young and, yet, you have accomplished so much. This resort seems to be a grand success, your wife is a lovely person, and you now have a child on the way. You really have it all, don't you!"

"It wasn't easy. I've worked my ass off to get here. And, to tell the truth, I'm scared to death."

"Of what?" Her eyes were large with wonderment.

"Of having a little soul to be responsible for. Of being too consumed with my work to pay enough attention to my wife. Of making a wrong decision that could destroy my financial security. And most of all, of losing everything I have here because of the economy going bust. And then there's my family back in the states that I never see, and my brother rotting away in a jail cell for something I know he couldn't have done." He became despondent as he stared into the flames, lost in his fear. Then as quickly as he had slipped into it, he bounced back. "Hey, let's hear about the happy honeymooners. Is everything okay with your accommodations here at the lodge so far?"

"Perfect." Her genuine smile told him that she meant it. "And Justin, don't worry. You've got the entire world at your feet and it's because you worked to achieve it all. You're not going to lose it now. You're much too smart for that."

"You're right. But I do worry about not having enough time for my family."

"That will come. This is still a new venture. Give it time. One day your wife and child will thank you for providing them with such a terrific life."

"You know what? It's kind of nice having a little sister to boost my morale. Thanks, Sis."

That night, as Nathan was showering for bed, she thought about what Justin had said about Collin not committing the crime for which he was being punished. *Could he be right? Could Collin possibly be innocent?* She decided that when she got a chance, she would send Collin a letter. She felt guilty that she hadn't gone to see him or contacted him at all. She'd let her own uncertainty keep her from doing a simple common courtesy.

Collin hadn't received much mail since he'd been incarcerated and was surprised when his name was called during mail call. He ambled over to the guard and retrieved the single envelope. The foreign stamps immediately cued him that it was from Austria—of course, Justin. There had been a time when a letter from Justin would have angered him, but now he was grateful that there was someone that cared enough to send him a letter. He really did love Justin. He always had. He just let his jealousy of him get in the way.

He waited until he was alone in his cell, then took the envelope from his pocket and opened it. To his surprise, it wasn't Justin's handwriting. Quickly glancing at the back page, he found the signature. 'Rachel'. His heart began to pound, and tears filled his eyes as he sat, stunned, onto his bunk.

'Dear Collin,

I am so sorry that I have avoided coming to see you or writing to you. I have no excuse except that I didn't know what to say to you. It's just so hard to come to grips with all that has happened.

I suppose you heard that Nathan and I got married. We are in Austria on our honeymoon. The landscape is so fabulous; I can hardly believe such a beautiful place actually exists. Justin has been wonderful to us. I want you to know, in case he hasn't told you himself, that he sincerely believes in your innocence.

He is devastated by the thought of you being in that prison. Did you hear about the baby? Trisha is due to deliver at any moment. In fact, by the time you get this letter, the baby will probably already be born.

Take care, and I promise to visit when I get home.

Rachel.'

He stared at the letter, reread it, and slowly folded it and slipped it back into its envelope. She would never be able to know just how much it meant to him to receive this very special gift.

Rachel puttered around in the kitchen attempting to get acquainted with her new home. Nathan's house was small and still gave the impression of a bachelor pad. She studied her surroundings, trying to visualize the changes she could make to make it feel more like her own home.

Nathan had gone to work, even though it was Sunday. There was a lot of catching up to do after being away on their honeymoon. His partner had tried to keep the construction on the Chavis' home progressing but the weather had not been cooperative. Today was bright and sunny, a perfect day to grade the yard that had been disturbed during construction. The house was almost complete, and Rachel couldn't wait to see it. She decided to fix a basket lunch and take it to her husband at the jobsite.

The sun was directly overhead and extremely hot. A slight breeze was the only thing that made the humidity tolerable. Nathan smiled as she waved from the car window. He was busy operating a Bobcat front loader, filling in the ruts made by the heavy trucks and equipment. "Hey, look at this, Baby! This machine is one terrific piece of equipment! Watch!" He raised the dirt-filled bucket and wheeled around 180 degrees, grinning from ear to ear, watching for her reaction rather than paying attention to what he was doing. He realized too late that the bucket had risen as far as it could and was dumping the dirt on top of his head. Everyone on the jobsite began chuckling, and Rachel couldn't help but join in the fun, at her husband's expense. There were painters hanging out of the windows and concrete laborers doubled over cackling. He turned the machine off and climbed down to greet his bride, his face red with embarrassment.

She tried hard to keep from snickering, "Are you okay?" She clamped her lips together to conceal the smirk that was trying to escape.

"I'm fine, and you can go ahead and laugh along with everyone else. I'm sure I won't hear the end of this one for a long time." His eyes twinkled as he put his arm around her shoulders and walked with her toward the house. "Come on in and see what we've done."

It was a bit eerie walking back into the place she'd called home when Lucille had been alive. It was as if she were revisiting the past; almost the same forlorn uneasiness she'd experienced when she'd gone home to clean out her mother's belongings in Wapiti. Nathan had done a terrific job duplicating the old house. Everything looked exactly the same, only fresh and new. Rachel's emotions were confused, ranging from extreme delight to utter sorrow.

"So what do you think?"

It was obvious he was fishing for praise, so wanting her to be proud of him. "You've done a great job, dear. It's exactly the same as it was." She walked slowly through the rooms, recalling every detail of how it had been; where the furniture had been placed, the color of the area rugs, the pictures on the mantel. She could almost picture her father sitting in his recliner in the study and Lucille puttering about from the kitchen to the dining room. Her heart was heavy, and there seemed to be a hole somewhere deep within her.

Nathan, noticing her disheartened mood, grabbed her hand and pulled her into his arms. "Did I see a basket in the car?"

Shaking herself back into the present, she nodded. "Yes, I brought sandwiches and thought we could have a picnic, if you want."

"Sounds great! I'm starving."

The prison walls were closing in on him. It was Sunday afternoon; surely someone would come to visit him. That was the only thing he had to look forward to. But he knew that everyone 'on the outside' was busy living their hectic lives and that he was just a passing thought in their minds every now and then. He might as well be dead as far as anyone was concerned. *I should be dead rather than my mother. I don't deserve to live. And she didn't deserve to die.*

"Hey, pretty boy. You've got a visitor. A real knock-out, too." The guards were almost as bad as the inmates. None of them gave him a break.

He was led to the visitation room where he sat on one side of a long metal table, and his 'guests' would be led in the room to sit on the opposite side. The number one rule was that there was to be absolutely no physical contact. A guard stood close by to be sure the rule was strictly enforced.

Melissa wasn't what he would consider a 'knock-out', but the sleazy guard might think so. She was the only female that came to see him that might be described that way. *It certainly couldn't be Aunt Marty.* He smiled at the thought.

The door opened. His heart began to race as Rachel appeared, like an angel swooping down to save him from hell. He stood and started to take a step toward her, but the guard stepped between them and ordered him back to his seat.

She stopped just inside the doorway and was trying hard to hide her dismay. Collin looked so thin and pale. The mischief was absent from his eyes, and his beard was scruffy. He looked twenty years older than he was, and even the broad smile on his face couldn't hide his misery. "Hi, Collin." She felt guilt-ridden for not visiting him sooner.

What do I say to her? I love you, Rachel. I'm so happy to see you, Rachel. Anything I say will sound lame. So he didn't say anything, but just waited for her to begin the conversation.

She walked to the table and took a seat. "I'm sorry I didn't come see you earlier. I just didn't know how to handle the situation."

"What situation is that? You mean, my being a murderer and all?"

She glanced down at the table trying to figure out how to answer. When she looked back up, he grinned at her, and she saw that familiar gleam in his eyes.

"It's okay, Rachel. I understand why you didn't come. But you are here now, so tell me how you're doing?"

"Well, did you get my letter?"

"Yes, I did." Suddenly he remembered that she was married to Nathan, and his heart ached from the thought. "So how's my old buddy Nathan doing?" *As if I really care.*

"He's great. He's working hard trying to finish the house for your fa—, for Raymond." She felt uncomfortable again. She didn't know how he felt about her father now or how he would feel about the house being rebuilt after he'd burned it down.

"I still think of him as my father, Rachel. I always will. I'm really glad the house is being reconstructed, but I—" He thought better of what he was about to say.

"But what?"

"Nothing. So tell me about Justin. Has the baby arrived yet?"

"Yes, Trisha went into labor right after I wrote to you. She had a beautiful little girl. They named her Lucille Colleen."

Total shock. That was the only way she could describe the look on Collin's face. "But why?"

"After your mother and you, of course."

"I know, but why would they do that?"

"Collin, they love you, and they wanted you to know how much. They believe in you and your innocence. I guess this is their way of conveying that to the world."

"And what about you?"

Oh God, now what do I say? "What do you mean?" *Stall until I figure out a good answer.*

"I mean do you believe I'm innocent? Or has your loving husband convinced you I did it?" The sarcasm about Nathan angered her.

"Look, I don't know what to believe. And you don't even seem to remember that night, according to your own testimony. So how do you know you didn't do it?"

He looked hurt, the pain appearing in his eyes. He looked away and spoke softly. "I just know." He stood. "Guard, I'm ready to go back to my cell now." His sorrowful gaze returned to her. He stared at her for a few minutes, memorizing her beautiful face. "I loved you, Rachel. I still do. I'm sorry you don't have more faith in me, but I understand. I could never deserve you." He started to walk toward the steel door where the guard waited.

"That's not true, Collin. I want to believe you, I really do." The tears poured down her cheeks, and she sobbed uncontrollably after the steel door slammed shut, and he was gone.

Another guard appeared and, taking her by the arm, led her from the room. "Don't cry for him, Honey. He ain't worth it. He's a loser, a murderer, a bum. You can do a lot better than the likes of him."

That evening when she told Nathan that she had visited the jail, he was furious. "I never want you to go back there again, do you hear?"

She was stunned by his tone. "Excuse me? I am not a child to be ordered around. If I want to go to visit the jail, I will go. Why are you so threatened by that?"

"I'm not threatened. It's just that a prison is no place for a respectable young woman to be hanging out. And I will not have a wife of mine being seen there visiting her old boyfriend." He slammed the rolled up newspaper down on the coffee table and glared at her.

"So you're jealous, is that it?"

"No, I'm not jealous. Why should I be jealous of a low-life murderer?"

"Then why are you being so unreasonable?"

He took a deep breath and closed his eyes, trying to calm himself. "All right. Let's see if you can understand simple English. First, you are my wife. Second, I'm trying to establish a business in this town and be a respected member of the upper class. And third, I don't want everyone gossiping about my beautiful wife visiting a murderer in prison. Why don't you understand that?"

She mimicked his sarcasm. "Well first, I'm your wife, and not your daughter. Second, I'm a highly respected model and an upstanding member of society in my own right, thank you very much. And third, I really don't care about the small-minded gossips in this town. I still think of Collin as a member of my family, and there are plenty of people that believe he is innocent."

"Innocent?! How could you believe he's innocent? How much evidence do you need?"

"I didn't say I believe he's innocent. I really don't know what to think."

Realizing that the he-man approach wasn't going to convince her, he decided to use a softer sell. He reached for her hand and gently pulled her toward him. He kissed her forehead and placed his finger under her chin, tilting her face up to his until their eyes locked. "Okay, I'm sorry I got so upset. I just want us to be able to put the past behind us and begin a fairy-tale life together. We can have it all, Sweetheart. But only if we're careful not to ruin our good name around town. We can have everyone eating out of our hands. This job rebuilding the Chavis house is going to launch me as the best builder around, not to mention putting a lot of dollars in the bank." His face was bright with excitement over their future. "Nothing can stop us if we play our cards right!"

She was seeing a greedy side of her husband that wasn't very appealing. Yet, she understood. It wasn't that long ago that she'd felt the same way. She had even plotted to marry Monroe Milliken so she could be an icon in the community. She smiled at her own stupidity.

Seeing her smile, Nathan mistook it for acceptance. "So you understand, right?"

Not wanting to continue this confusing quarrel, she nodded and, turning away from him, marched determinedly toward the bedroom. *I understand, but that doesn't mean I agree.*

"So where are you going?"

"To take a shower." As the water rained over her, it cooled her reddened face and washed away the saltiness of the tears.

CHAPTER 17

Tuesday, January 8

The holidays had been a whirlwind of excitement for everyone except Rachel. She'd been so busy organizing the elaborate parties that her husband insist they give, she hadn't had time to enjoy any of it. There'd been the spirited masquerade ball for Halloween, then the enormous dinner party and dance for Thanksgiving, and the extravagant Christmas gala. Then to top it all off, they'd thrown the most elegant New Year's Eve bash complete with fireworks.

Thank God it's all over for a while. She'd just finished boxing the last of the Christmas ornaments and was sprawled on the sofa for a much needed nap. In front of her was a coffee table where the newspapers lay stacked one upon the other. Nathan wouldn't allow her to throw any of them away. He wanted to save each and every article that had been printed praising their successful social events. 'Mr. and Mrs. Nathan Hamilton were the most beautiful and successful couple in town', according to the society pages, and her husband was enjoying every moment of glory he could squeeze from it.

Well, Rachel, you wanted to be one of the elite, and here you are. She looked up. "Momma, you always warned me to be careful what I wished for. You were so right."

When she awoke from her nap, the room was completely dark. She slowly sat up on the sofa and reached for the lamp switch. The bright light burned her eyes, and it took a few seconds for her to focus on the clock. It was almost 1:00 in the morning. She crept quietly into the bedroom. The moonlight was enough light for her to see that the bed had never been turned down. Obviously, Nathan had not yet come home. *Where could he be?* She closed the heavy draperies, turned down the covers on the bed, put on her nightgown and climbed between the cold, lonely sheets. She was beginning to get used to his late nights 'out with the guys'. He claimed it was just a few harmless poker games, but she'd noticed their savings account balance had been dropping rapidly.

Nathan crept into the room, trying hard not to awaken her. But as he began removing his pants, she roused enough to ask him what time it was.

"Shhh. It's about 1:00. Go back to sleep, Honey." He slipped under the covers and lay still until he was sure she'd gone back to sleep.

All of a sudden she sat up and began climbing out of the bed.

"Where are you going?"

"I have to go to the bathroom." Before he could stop her, she opened the door to their bathroom, and sunlight filled the room. "I thought you said it was only 1:00! Where have you been all night?"

"Jerry's. We had a little too much to drink, and I didn't want to drive until I slept it off some. So I slept on his sofa."

"What is going on with you? This isn't even the weekend, and you're staying out drinking all night. How do you expect to run your business when you're drunk all the time?"

"I'm not drunk all the time, for Christ's sake. I just got a little carried away last night, that's all."

Shaking her head, she went to the kitchen and turned on the coffee maker, then proceeded to the bathroom for a shower. By the time she returned to the bedroom, Nathan had dressed and gone.

She straightened the house and made the bed, thinking about Nathan and Collin. They'd been friends, almost like brothers, most of their lives, but now there was so much animosity between them. She knew that Collin had been somewhat jealous of her and Nathan, but why would Nathan be so angry with Collin? The more she thought about it, the more she felt that the problem was much deeper than just a simple rivalry over her.

She picked up Nathan's watch from the nightstand. *So, you were in such a hurry, you forgot your watch.* She opened the top drawer of the nightstand and placed the watch among his other jewelry and small trinkets. She fondly picked through some of the items that had special meaning to him. There was his father's pocket watch that no longer worked, but he kept it because it had been his father's. And there was the birthday card she had given him, along with a small souvenir paperweight they'd gotten on their honeymoon at the ski lodge. Moving the items around, she noticed his mother's ring, still on the chain, pushed into the back corner of the drawer. She pulled it out and held it up, remembering the day she'd found it among the ashes. An odd feeling came over her, as if there was something more about this ring that she needed to know. She tried to shake off the sensation and quickly placed the jewelry back in its little corner of the drawer so he wouldn't know she'd been snooping. Then she retreated to the attic to tackle putting away the decorations and Christmas boxes in an orderly manner.

While moving the storage boxes around to make room for the new ornaments and artificial Christmas tree, she noticed some of the boxes were labeled. One large box was marked "Father's things", and another was marked "Mother's things". Since Nathan had told her very little about his parents, she was rather curious about them. Feeling like a thief in the night, she carefully opened his father's box first. There were a few articles of clothing, including a suede hat, a number of books, mostly manuals about construction and architecture, and a couple of ledger books with job costs and sales figures. She flipped through one of them, and a piece of paper fell to the floor. It was an envelope with a letter inside. Suddenly, she had a feeling of déjà vu. The memory of another letter she'd found among her mother's things swept over her. That letter had changed her world completely. And now, as she held this one, she had the same ominous sensation that she'd experienced that day. *But that's silly. This letter is probably nothing at all.* She looked at the envelope. It was addressed to Mr. Lawrence Hamilton, and there was no return address. She opened it and began reading. It was a short note from a woman that was telling him good-bye. A typical 'Dear John' letter, or in this case 'Dear Larry'. And it was simply signed "L." Nathan had told her that his mother had left them when he'd been very young, so she assumed that this was probably from her. She rummaged through the box, but found nothing else of interest.

Then she opened his mother's box. She found a few articles of clothing, a small broken trinket box, and some costume jewelry. She started to put the clothing back when she noticed a book resting flat in the bottom of the box. It was a dark color, and the lighting was dim, so she'd almost overlooked it. She reached down and picked it up, realizing as she opened it that it was a diary. Feeling wickedly evil, she put it aside to read later and replaced all the other things back into the box. She quickly shoved all the new ornaments and boxes along the edge of the attic wall and carried the diary downstairs with her. She was ready to settle down to read it when she heard Nathan's key in the front door. She thrust the book under the sofa and pretended to be asleep.

He bent over her and gently brushed her hair back. "Rachel, Sweetheart, I'm home."

She roused slowly and stretched, speaking sleepily. "Hi—How was your day?" She propped herself up and looked around. "What time is it?"

"It's only three thirty. I took off a little early today."

"I guess you're tired after your night out last night." She hadn't intended it to sound like she were nagging or complaining, but that's how he took it.

He shook his head, disgust showing on his face. "Actually, I came home early so I could spend some time with you, but I guess that was a mistake."

"I'm sorry, I didn't mean that the way it sounded."

"Yeah, right." He stomped into the kitchen and grabbed a beer from the fridge. When he returned, his mood had improved. "So, what did you do today?"

"I straightened up the attic and organized the Christmas ornaments and boxes. It was such a mess up there that it took me the better part of the day."

"You should just throw it all up there and forget it. It is just an attic. There's no need for it to be so organized."

"Next year when we have to get it all out again, you'll appreciate it being easy to find."

He picked up the newspaper and began reading, but she grabbed it from him. "Oh, no you don't, Buster. You said you came home to spend time with me."

He smiled and grabbed her arm, pulling her into his lap. "Okay, you. What would you like to do?"

"Talk."

"Talk about what?"

"Well, when I was in the attic, I found a couple of boxes. One was your dad's things, and the other was your mother's. It just made me realize how little you've told me about your parents."

"Not much to tell. Mother left when I was too young to know what was happening. And Dad passed away just a few years ago. What more would you like to know?"

"Well, what was your mother's name?"

"Suzanne."

Suzanne! That means that letter wasn't from her after all. So who was it from? She tried to hide her surprise. "Why do you think she left like she did?"

He shrugged. "Who knows. I guess she just wasn't cut out to be a wife and mother."

"No, I believe there had to have been a reason other than that."

"Probably, but I really don't want to talk about her. Let's change the subject."

That night after he'd gone to sleep, she lay awake wondering about the letter. She slipped from beneath the covers and crept back into the living room, pulled the diary from under the sofa, and began to read. The first fifteen or twenty pages were typical daily reports, nothing major or exciting. She was about the put it down when she noticed an entry dated May 20.

'I saw them today. They were in each other's arms acting like teen-age lovers. I wonder if Raymond knows about them. His pretty little high-society

wife acting like the town slut with my husband.'

The entries after that described numerous times that Suzanne had watched her husband with this other woman and how she ached from the painful betrayal. Rachel's heart pounded in her ears as she began putting pieces together. Lucille's name hadn't been written yet, but everything was pointing that way. And her father had told her that Lucille had had an affair with Collin's father. And the letter, signed 'L.' It was all beginning to make sense.

But if this is true, then that would make Nathan and Collin half brothers! She wondered if Nathan knew.

Five months had passed since her last visit to the prison. When Collin entered the visiting area, she was relieved to see him looking physically fit and more like his old self. The little boy was gone and had been replaced by this hard, masculine person standing before her. Her heart raced, and the blood rushed to her face as her groin throbbed. His virility took her breath away, and she found that she couldn't speak.

He approached the table and sat staring at her like a vulture about to devour its prey. "So, what brings you here?"

"I needed to see you."

"Why?"

She ached to tell him that she had never stopped loving him, but she had to control herself. "I've learned something, and I wanted to discuss it with you."

"What?" He seemed very detached and disinterested.

"It concerns your mother."

He took a deep breath and softened a bit as he looked down at the table. "What about her?"

She swallowed, trying to build up her nerve. "Well, Dad told us that she had an affair, but he never told us with whom. I think I have discovered who it was."

He looked disgusted. "What difference does it make? It was so many years ago, what could it possibly matter today?"

"Normally I would agree with you, but aren't you just a bit curious who your father is?"

"Raymond Chavis is my father. He's all the father I need. I really don't care who got my mother pregnant. It just doesn't matter."

"But it might. If what I suspect is true, then you may have a brother, other than Justin."

"And why should I care about that?"

"Because it's Nathan." She sat waiting for a response.

"Nathan will never be my brother, no matter if his father did screw my mother." His bitterness toward Nathan was stronger than she had ever imagined. His eyes were full of hatred, and his jaws began to pulsate as he ground his teeth together. "Is that the only thing you wanted to discuss?" He stood as if dismissing her.

"No, please sit down." She begged with her eyes, and he couldn't refuse her.

He sat back down, his attitude softened. "So what else?"

"Nothing. I just want to know about how you are?"

"Hmmph. I'm just great. This place is a real blast." His sarcasm made her feel a little foolish for asking.

"I'm sorry. I just want you to know that I do care. I would do anything to get you out of this disgusting place."

Suddenly, his demeanor changed completely as he leaned toward her, startled. "Are you serious?"

"Of course. Did you honestly think I didn't care?"

"Well, you haven't exactly been a frequent visitor since I've been here."

"I know. But I haven't forgotten what we meant to each other. Those kind of feelings don't just vanish."

He smiled for the first time, and again she felt her pulse quicken. "Yeah, I dream about those days a lot. Those memories are all I have in here."

There was silence as they looked at each other and both silently remembered. She suddenly looked down at her wedding band and reminded herself that she was a married woman and had to bring herself back into the present reality. "I think maybe I should be going."

"No, please don't. Tell me what it is you suspect about my mother. I want to know." *Anything to keep you from leaving now.*

Remembering why she had come, she recounted all that she'd discovered. When she finished, he shook his head.

"It sure doesn't sound like a lot of evidence. That's about as circumstantial as the bullshit that landed me in here! Nathan is a real piece of work, isn't he?!"

"What do you mean?"

"I mean that you have been taken in by the best con I've ever met, including all the ones in this jail. All that man cares about is manipulating everyone and everything to get what he wants. You'd better take a closer look at your loving husband." He stood up and motioned to the guard. "Good luck, Honey, you're going to need it. Come back when you've figured it out, okay?" As he disappeared through the steel door, she sat motionless, confused by his remarks.

Driving home, she realized there was one person she could turn to that might have some of the answers. A short time later, she arrived at the mill house.

Black smoke rose from the flue indicating fresh firewood had been added to the old wood stove. *Good, she's home!*

They sat at the kitchen table as the older woman poured cups of hot tea and offered Rachel a muffin. "What's on your mind, child? You look so frazzled."

"I need to know if you have any idea who the man was that Lucille had an affair with?"

"And why would that matter to you?"

"Well, for one thing, this man would be Collin's father."

"And?"

Rachel looked her squarely in the eye, determined to find out the truth. "Do you know who he was or not?"

"I might. But I don't see why it is of concern to you. Maybe you should tell me why you're asking."

She sat back and closed her eyes, feeling defeated. How could she possibly explain why she needed to know, when she didn't quite understand why it was so important to her herself. "Maybe you're right. Maybe it's not important at all. But I just have this nagging feeling that it could be."

"Okay, let's start by you telling me what caused you to come to this point. What is it that started you thinking about Lucille and this man?"

"A diary I found in our attic. It was Nathan's mother's. I also found a letter to Larry Hamilton that was signed 'L'."

"I see." Aunt Marty rose from her chair and walked to the sink, her back to Rachel. She remained quiet, as if in deep thought.

"So does this mean anything to you?"

Aunt Marty turned and leaned against the counter. "I don't see any reason to hide the truth any longer. Yes, Lucille had an affair with Larry."

"So Lawrence Hamilton was Collin's father?"

"Yes. Collin and Nathan are half brothers."

"And neither of them knows this?"

"No. At least as far as I know they don't."

"Do you think they should be told?"

"I don't see what good that would do, dear. It would just re-open old wounds and cause a lot of heartache and confusion. Raymond doesn't even know. It may devastate him to find out."

Rachel thought about what she'd said. Maybe she was right. "I just came from seeing Collin, and I told him about the diary and the letter." She was a bit sheepish as she peeked at Marty, afraid she had already done something wrong.

"And how did he react?"

"He didn't believe it. He said my evidence was too flimsy, just like the evidence that had put him behind bars."

"He's right. He shouldn't be in that jail. There wasn't enough proof of his guilt for him to have been found guilty."

"So, you still don't believe he did it?"

"No. Collin would never do such a thing. I knew that boy better than almost anyone, besides his mother, and there just isn't a mean bone in his body. Sure he was mischievous, but he wasn't bad. It would take an evil person to set a house on fire knowing there were people inside. Besides that, Collin loved his mother, and he loved you, more than life itself. He just wouldn't have done it."

"But what about the evidence?"

"What evidence?!" She had spat out the two words in disgust.

"Well, there was the gas can with his finger-prints on it found behind the steel mill. And the fact that he went to Nathan's and was drunk, angry and threatening. Then he testified that he couldn't remember if he had done it or not. What are we suppose to make of that?"

"I don't know, but I do know that he didn't do it. I have my theories that I'm working on proving, but I'd rather not discuss them with you right yet. I hope you understand."

"Of course." She felt closer to Aunt Marty than any other woman she knew, and she really needed someone to confide in. "Aunt Marty, could I talk to you about something else?"

Seeing the desperation, Aunt Marty smiled reassuringly. "Of course, dear. What is it?"

"It's my marriage."

The older woman sat back down at the table and reached over to pat her arm. "You seemed so happy at the beautiful parties you gave. Are you having problems?"

"Well, not really. It's just that Nathan isn't acting like the man I thought I married."

Aunt Marty laughed. "They never do. Once they have that wedding band on your finger, they change over night. It's as if someone turns on a switch that tells them they can become pure assholes now."

Rachel laughed with her. "You sound like you speak from experience. Were you ever married?"

"Lord, no. I saw too many other people go through this situation. I learned from their mistakes. I date and enjoy men, but I never want anyone to tell me what I can or cannot do. So I just never committed to letting someone own me, body and soul."

She told her about Nathan's drinking and staying out late at night and about other little things that bothered her. Aunt Marty listened and joked with her, making her feel that her problems weren't nearly as big as she had first thought. That evening, she had a special candlelight dinner waiting for Nathan when he arrived home.

Her husband seemed to be back to his old lovable self for a couple of days, but it was short-lived. He became moody and irritable, and every time she saw him, he was either drinking, already drunk, or going out to get a drink. She'd been told by some of the models at work that his car had been seen at the local tavern, Benny's Pub, almost every night. She decided to pay him a surprise visit there.

She drove into the parking lot glancing at the clock on her dash. 12:50. Late enough that he was probably good and drunk by now. She scanned the parking lot. His car was right in front of the building. *He must have gotten here plenty early to get that parking space.*

She took a deep breath, reluctantly left the security of her car and walked through the entrance. The parking lot had been brightly lit, and the room was dark, so it took a few seconds for her eyes to adjust so she could scout him out.

Before she could spot him, one of the patrons yelled out, "Hey, Nathan, it's your squaw." Another man chimed in, "Yeah, Nate. Is it true that squaw's will do anything to make her man happy?"

There were hoots and laughter as she finally saw him sitting at a corner table. Rather than come to her rescue, he was laughing along with them and answered, "Sure, why do you think I married her?"

Another outburst of hysteria surrounded her. She wanted nothing more than to flee from the ridicule, but her anger drove her forward to confront her husband. She approached slowly, staring straight into his eyes. She reached his table, leaned toward him and smiled. "You know, love, there are some things in this life that I just cannot live without. And I'm here to tell you and your friends—You are NOT one of them."

She turned back toward the door and held her head high as she crossed the room. She noticed Melissa Evans leaning against the bar, smiling and giving her a thumbs up, but she didn't acknowledge her. She was too intent on making a quick exit.

She could hear Nathan's voice through the roar of the crowd, "Hey, where do you think you're going, Bitch?" But she ignored him and continued out the door.

As she reached her car, Melissa came racing across the parking lot. "Rachel, I need to talk to you about Nathan."

"Don't even try to take up for him. I'm not in the mood to listen."

"Oh, no, I wouldn't. But there are some things you need to know about him. It's important."

Nathan was stumbling through the tavern's door, so Rachel quickly unlocked the car doors. "Get in."

Melissa didn't hesitate. She climbed in, and they sped away, leaving him standing in the parking lot screaming obscenities.

"Okay, so what is it you wanted to tell me?" Rachel wasn't so sure she wanted to hear what this trollop had to say. She hadn't been impressed with her at the trial, and seeing her at the local bar hadn't improved her opinion.

"Well, I guess you know from the trial that I have a little girl."

Rachel nodded.

"Well, what you don't know is that my ex isn't her father."

Rachel immediately flashed back to the trial. Melissa had sworn under oath that the child's father was her ex-husband. *So she was protecting Collin after all.* She stared straight ahead and continued to drive, trying not to show any emotion.

"It's hard for me to tell you this, you being Nathan's wife and all. But Nathan is my little girl's father."

Rachel went into shock, outwardly showing no reaction. She couldn't believe what she was hearing. When she arrived at her home, she didn't remember how she had gotten there. She couldn't recall making any turns. She'd just driven on automatic pilot. "Please come on in. I think I need to hear this whole story."

Melissa followed her inside and continued to explain. "Nathan had made me promise, back when I got pregnant, that no one could ever know that he was the father. He was worried that it would ruin his chances of becoming the successful businessman around town. So I agreed that I would tell everyone that my ex was the father. Nathan has been helping financially by giving me money every now and then, but he swore me to secrecy about that too."

"So why are you telling me all this now?"

"Well, because something happened last week, and I didn't know what else to do."

"What happened?" Rachel was beginning to get frustrated about having to drag this story out of her.

"Nathan never comes to visit much, but when he does, he calls himself 'Uncle Nate' to our daughter. Last week, when he came to visit, I wasn't home. I had left her with a sitter while I was at work."

Suddenly, Rachel remembered a news report she had heard. "Wait. Evans. Is your daughter's name Stacy?"

"That's right."

"Didn't I hear on the news that your daughter had been abused by her sitter, and the sitter had been arrested for it?"

"Yeah, but she didn't do it."

"So, what happened?"

"Nathan had come over, and the sitter left to go pick up some things at the store while he watched my little girl. After she returned, he was anxious to leave. The sitter noticed that Stacy was acting a little more quiet than usual. She called me at work and said she was concerned, that Stacy wasn't acting right. When I got home, she was leaning over my little girl trying to give her mouth-to-mouth. The paramedics got there just after I did and took over." Her eyes had watered, and her voice was beginning to quiver.

"So how is Stacy now?"

"She's still in the hospital, but the doctors think she'll be okay. She still hasn't said anything, so we're still waiting for her to respond. They really won't know if there is any permanent damage until she shows some kind of reaction. She just lays there, staring." Melissa began to sob uncontrollably as Rachel tried to comfort her.

After a few minutes, Rachel went to the kitchen to get some iced tea, hoping to give Melissa a chance to collect herself. When she returned, the young mother seemed to have her emotions under control. Rachel waited patiently as they sipped their tea, trying not to push too hard for the answers to her many questions.

Melissa continued without any prodding. "Anyway, I believe the sitter when she says she didn't do anything. I think Nathan may have lost his patience with Stacy and struck her or shook her, causing damage to her brain, and it only showed up later after the sitter got home. That's why he was in such a big hurry to leave."

"But you don't know that is what happened. What would make you think that Nathan would do such a thing, and not the sitter?"

"I've seen Nathan's temper. It's not a pretty sight. And I've known the sitter for a long time. She adores Stacy and has never even raised her voice to her that I know of. She's just a calm, easy-going person."

Unfortunately, Rachel had seen Nathan's temper too. And with the added influence of alcohol lately, none of this story surprised her. It also explained why his money was dwindling faster than she believed it should have been. She'd thought he was just gambling it away, but maybe he was using it to help support his child.

"Well, this is quite a revelation for me to absorb. I need some time to think about it all and decide what we should do. But for right now, let's get you back to your car."

"Yeah, I need to get back to the hospital. I just needed to get away from there for a while, so I came to Benny's for a drink hoping it would help me rest better. It's so hard to sleep at the hospital, but I need to be near my little girl so I've been staying there day and night."

"If you believe Nathan did this, why hasn't he been arrested?"

"I don't have any proof. It's just what I think happened."

CHAPTER 18

Monday, January 14

After taking Melissa back to the bar to retrieve her car, Rachel returned home. She rushed through the house, nervously grabbing anything she would need for the next few days, trying desperately to be gone before Nathan could get home. Suitcase packed, she glanced around once more, peaked outside to be sure he hadn't arrived yet, and hurried to the car.

Once out of sight of the house, she slowed down, pondering if she should go to the Chavis house or to Aunt Marty's. Driving past the beautiful reconstructed home, her heart pounding with apprehension, she decided it would be easier to talk to Aunt Marty about this situation.

When she reached the quaint old mill house, she sat in the driveway dreading waking the older woman at such a late hour. It was 3:00 in the morning.

Just then, a light came on in the house, and a few seconds later, Aunt Marty appeared at the front porch, shotgun in hand.

Rachel quickly opened the car door, allowing the dome light to reveal her identity to the frightened woman.

"Lord, child, what are you doing out there this time of night?"

"I need some place to stay and someone I can trust to talk to. I was hoping you could help me."

Hearing the desperation in her voice, Aunt Marty motioned for her to come in. "Well, don't just sit out there in the dark. Get in here and start talking."

By the time Rachel reached the kitchen, Aunt Marty was already fixing the coffee. Coffee-maker gurgling, the older woman sat down at the table and motioned for Rachel to do the same. "Okay, tell old Marty what's eatin' at you."

Rachel related the entire story that Melissa had told her about her little girl.

"Yes, I know about little Stacy. I've been to the hospital to see her. She has definitely been traumatized, no doubt about that."

"But do you honestly think Nathan could do such a thing?"

"Maybe you need to ask him."

"He would never admit to it even if he did it."

"Maybe, maybe not. When a person drinks, he will sometimes admit to things he might normally try to hide. A drunk doesn't think about the consequences the way a sober person would."

Rachel slept through most of the next day, making up for her lack of sleep the night before. At 4:00, she went to the hospital to see how Stacy was doing. Stepping from the elevator, she thought she saw Nathan entering the door to the stairway.

Melissa was standing outside the door of her daughter's room and smiled when she spotted Rachel approaching. "The doctor is in there examining her now. She seems to be a little better today. She smiled at me and said 'Hi, Mommy'." Tears rolled down both cheeks.

The doctor exited the room. "Everything looks much more promising today. I want to keep a close eye on her for a while, but I'm extremely optimistic." His calm voice and his reassuring smile made them all feel that Stacy was going to be just fine.

Melissa grabbed Rachel and hugged her. She'd been so worried for so long that now her body almost collapsed from fatigue and hunger. Rachel led her to a group of chairs, and the doctor had the nurse bring her a cup of juice. After a few minutes, she recovered.

Rachel was still thinking about the figure she'd seen headed to the stairway when she arrived. "Did I see Nathan leaving when I got here?"

"Yeah, he was here." Melissa almost spat the words. "Pretending to be all concerned, but not concerned enough to tell the truth!" She was understandably bitter.

Later that night, Rachel drove past the tavern and, just as she expected, Nathan's truck was parked in its usual spot. She then went back to their home to wait for him. While she waited, she collected as many of her belongings as possible and packed them into her car. She also made sure she had the letter she had found among Lawrence Hamilton's effects, Suzanne Hamilton's diary, and the diamond ring on the chain.

Nathan stumbled in a little after 2:00 AM. "So you're home," he muttered. "Where the hell were you last night?"

"I went over to Aunt Marty's and stayed the night."

"You weren't at work today either. I tried to call you. They told me you were sick."

"That's right." *Sick of you.* "But I'm better now." She stood up and started to the kitchen. "Would you like some coffee or a drink?" She was trying to get him to relax his guard.

"No, I don't want anything. I just need to go to bed." He staggered into the bedroom with Rachel following him. She helped him remove his clothes and pulled the covers down, then tucked him in as if he were a child.

He smiled up at her. "Thanks, Babe. You always take such good care of me."

"Of course, you're my husband. That's what I'm suppose to do." *Because I'm a good little squaw.* She wanted to choke his tongue out, but knew she would get further by pretending to be the loving wife. "Sweetheart, why didn't you tell me about your daughter, Stacy?"

"My daughter?" He didn't show much emotion.

"Yes, your daughter. She's such a beautiful little girl. I went to see her at the hospital today."

He looked through her, as if in a trance. "Yeah, the doc says she's getting better. She's gonna be okay." A tear gathered in the corner of his eye.

"I'm sure you didn't mean to hurt her, it was just an accident." She tried to sound compassionate and stroked his hair back lovingly.

He reached out and embraced her, desperately holding onto her for comfort. "You're right, I never meant to hurt her. She just kept crying for her mommy, and I couldn't stand it anymore. All I did was shake her a little bit to try to shut her up, she went limp for a minute, and then she stopped crying." Rachel had pulled back and was looking down at him. He stared back at her as if he really couldn't comprehend what had happened. He was like a confused, blubbering child. Then he suddenly pushed her away, his temper flaring. "The bitch should never have gotten pregnant to begin with. If she had used birth control like she's supposed to, none of this would've happened. I never wanted no brat kid. At least if the kid had died, I wouldn't have to pay that bitch no more money."

Rachel had heard enough. She grabbed her purse and keys and ran out of the house. *This man is a monster.* Not only had he caused his own child to almost die, he was willing to let an innocent woman go to prison for what he'd done. Suddenly a thought shivered through her. *My God, I don't even know my own husband! Could this be what Collin was trying to warn me about?*

When she arrived back at Aunt Marty's, the older woman was waiting for her. "So, how did it go?"

"Just as you thought. He told the whole truth. He was so drunk, he never realized what he was confessing." She pulled the tape recorder from her pocket and gave it to Aunt Marty.

Aunt Marty smiled and muttered "Now I've got him" as she took the tape from Rachel's quivering hand.

They sat at the kitchen table as Aunt Marty tried to explain to Rachel what she had been working on for weeks. "It was just a matter of piecing all the evidence together and figuring out just how Nathan had almost committed the perfect murder. This time I approached everything from a completely different angle. I listened carefully to the facts that Collin could remember about that night. Then I began piecing together where each and every person was at the time of the fire. The only person, besides Collin, that hadn't had an alibi was Nathan. So then I concentrated on a motive. That was the difficult part."

"So you've suspected Nathan all along?"

"No, I've just figured it all out in the past couple of weeks. I was so relieved when you started to see the darker side of him. I was worried about how I was going to approach this with you. You know, I've always thought there was something just not quite right about him, but never could put it into words. He was just too smooth to the point of becoming slippery."

Aunt Marty and Rachel became completely consumed with finding a way to prove Collin's innocence. After several months of careful study and investigation, they finally were able to accumulate enough new evidence to convince the courts to accept an appeal for Collin's case, but this time Aunt Marty would act as his defense attorney.

Monday, April 8

Reporters and curious on-lookers swarmed the courthouse, and the commotion was so loud, one had to scream to be heard above them.

After Mr. Benton, the prosecuting attorney, had completed his opening remarks, Aunt Marty opted to forego her opening speech and get on with the trial. It had been her experience that giving an opening statement only benefitted the other lawyer by disclosing the plan of defense. Judges and jurors were always anxious to hear real evidence rather than a lot of theories, so she won points with them while keeping the opposition ignorant of her strategy. This served to unnerve most prosecutors.

During the first three days of the trial, Mr. Benton presented his case in much the same way that Ms. Avery had in the first trial. No new evidence and no surprises. It had worked the first time, and he still felt it was a strong case. Now all he could do was try to block Mayor Shaw from negating his efforts.

Aunt Marty felt an overwhelming sense of satisfaction as she rose to begin her defense. She began with her main target, Nathan Hamilton. The time had finally come for her to face him. She waited for him to be sworn in and began her attack. "Mr. Hamilton, did you go back to the property after the night of the fire?"

"Of course. My company helped Mr. Chavis rebuild."

"Is it common practice to use a metal-detector to search a piece of property prior to rebuilding a home?"

"No. I had lost something that had great sentimental value to me. I took a metal detector there to look for it."

"When do you think you lost this valuable item?"

"I thought I might have lost it the night of the fire when I went in to get Rachel and the Chavises out of the flames."

"Oh, yes, when you rescued Rachel. Tell us about that. How did you happen to be there?"

"I was worried about Rachel because Collin had said some threatening things." At this, the prosecutor looked smugly at the jurors. "So I drove by the house to make sure everything was okay. When I saw the house was on fire and I heard Rachel screaming for help, I ran in and got her out."

"You ran in the front door?"

"Yes. The fire was already too bad in the rear of the house. I had to hurry up the stairs and back down before it spread to the front."

"Let's get back to this item you lost. Did you find it?"

"I didn't, but Rachel did."

"Rachel. You mean the woman that is now your wife?"

"Yes."

"And did she find it on that property?"

"Yes, in the ashes."

"Where in the ashes? I mean, in what area of the house?"

"I don't know."

"I see." Aunt Marty hesitated and looked through her notes before proceeding. "What was this item that your wife found?"

"A ring on a chain."

"And why was this jewelry so important to you?"

"It was the only thing I had left of my mother."

"What happened to your mother?"

The prosecuting attorney had heard enough and jumped to his feet. "Objection, Your Honor. This line of questioning is going nowhere. What could what happened to Mr. Hamilton's mother possibly have to do with this case?"

Judge Carlisle looked at Aunt Marty over his glasses that rested on his nose. "Ms. Shaw, could you please get to your point quickly or I will have to agree with Mr. Benton."

"Yes, Your Honor. It will become clear very soon. May I proceed?"

"Go ahead. Objection over-ruled, at least for the moment."

Aunt Marty glanced at the jury and then re-worded her question. "Is your mother still alive, Mr. Hamilton?"

"I don't know. I haven't heard from her in a long time."

"How long?"

"Since I was a young boy. She left me and my father when I was five years old."

"Did your father ever give you an explanation as to why she left?"

"He didn't have to. I knew."

"And why was that?"

"Because my father had an affair, and she couldn't live with that."

Looking confused, Aunt Marty walked toward the jury, her back to Nathan. "Didn't you say you were only five years old when your mother left?"

"That's right."

"Yet, you were wise enough, even at that young age, to understand that your mother had left because your father was having an affair?"

"I had seen him with his lover. Even at that age, I knew it wasn't right."

"I see." This time she looked at him with compassion, as if he were still that five year old in pain from what he'd seen. "Nathan, did you know the woman that you had seen with your father?"

"Yes."

"Who was it?" She turned and looked at Raymond, sorrow clearly showing in her eyes, as she asked the question.

Nathan looked down and mumbled a name. The judge asked him to speak up so everyone could hear. "It was Lucille Chavis." The courtroom erupted, everyone gasping and expressing their surprise. Flashbulbs flickered and cameras whirred. The judge banged his gavel and demanded order. The prosecuting attorney rose to his feet and hollered over the commotion. "Objection! This is a ridiculous display which serves no purpose. I still do not see how this relates to this case."

The judge was finally able to gain control over the courtroom. "Mayor, I tend to agree with Mr. Benton. Please make your point or change your line of questioning."

"Please be patient, Your Honor. It's very complicated, but this all does tie into what happened the night of the fire, I assure you."

"Very well. Continue."

Nathan was beginning to get fidgety as Aunt Marty approached him once again. "You became very angry with Lucille over the years, didn't you Nathan?"

"No, not really." He shifted in his seat.

"Oh, come on. This woman tore your family apart, and you expect us to believe you didn't hate her?"

Nathan looked confused. His eyes shifted around the courtroom as if looking for someone to help him out.

"It's time to tell the truth, Nathan. Did you set the Chavis house on fire that night and frame Collin for it?"

Nathan stood up and looked vehemently at Aunt Marty. "NO! I did no such thing. Why would I wait over twenty years to get even? I got over it a long time ago. In fact, everyone knows that Mrs. Chavis was like a mother to me. Her son, Justin, was my best friend." He sat back in the witness chair and seemed to look pleased with his reasoning.

Marty looked thoughtful for a moment. "No more questions at this time, but I would like to reserve the right to recall this witness later."

Rachel sat in the center of the courtroom audience and studied Nathan's face as he was leaving the witness stand. He looked completely drained and unnerved. The judge dismissed the court for lunch, to reconvene at 2:00.

Everyone stood, and Collin turned to look at her. He was more handsome now than he'd ever been. He was in top physical condition from working out, and the bitterness had melted away. The sparkle had returned to those intense blue eyes.

CHAPTER 19

Thursday, April 11

At promptly 2:00, court reconvened, and Aunt Marty continued to present her case. "I would like to call Melissa Evans."
Melissa walked into the courtroom looking determined. She glared at Nathan as she walked past the pew where he was seated. As she was sworn in, Rachel noticed how good she looked. She had a new hairstyle and was dressed in an eggshell-colored business suit with matching pumps. She appeared to be a very respectable and self-assured woman, not at all like the shy, scared girl that had testified at the first trial.

"Ms. Evans, do you know both Collin Chavis and Nathan Hamilton?"
"Yes, very well."
"First, tell us what your relationship is with Collin Chavis."
"He's a very dear friend. He has always shown me respect and tried to help me whenever he could. Sometimes, he was the only one I could talk to that seemed to really understand and truly care."
"Was he ever anything more than a friend?"
"Not really."
"What do you mean?"
"Well, I really cared about him a lot, and would have liked it if we could've had a closer relationship, but he never loved me in that way."
"So, you never had a sexual relationship?"
"I didn't say that. We did sleep together occasionally, but it was more of a matter of just needing to be close to somebody, and we trusted each other and knew where we stood. So it was nice, but not a commitment or anything."
"And what about Nathan Hamilton. Tell us about your relationship with him."
"Well, Nathan and I got real close at one time. We had a regular thing going about two years ago."
"And what happened?"

"I got pregnant, but he didn't want no children. So he got really angry and wanted me to have an abortion. But I just couldn't do such a thing."

"So you had Nathan's baby?"

"Yes, and she's a beautiful little girl."

"Yes, she is. And how old is she now?"

"She's two years old."

"You had quite a scare a few months ago. Please tell us about that."

Mr. Benton jumped to his feet. "Objection, Your Honor. Where is this line of questioning going? I don't see what relevance this woman's child has to an arson case. I'm sure a two year old didn't have anything to do with the fire."

"Ms. Shaw?" The judge peeked over his reading glasses.

"Your Honor, I assure you that this is very pertinent to this case. I beg the court for its patience."

"Okay, proceed."

Rachel smiled. Aunt Marty reminded her of a female Colombo. She had watched the old detective show reruns with her father a few times. It was one of his favorites.

Aunt Marty nodded toward Melissa, "Go ahead."

"Well, I had gone to work and left Stacy, that's my little girl, with my sitter. Nathan decided to visit her, and while he was there, the sitter left to go get a few things from the store. She figured Nathan could watch Stacy for a little while. While she was gone, Stacy must have started crying and gotten on Nathan's nerves..."

"Objection. Ms. Evans wasn't even at home. She can't possibly know what happened."

"Sustained."

Defense Attorney Shaw had been waiting for that objection, and she was ready. "That's okay, Melissa. Did you receive a phone call at work that day concerning your daughter?"

"Yes. The sitter called me and told me Stacy wasn't acting just right so she had called 911 and was waiting for them to come. I rushed home and found Stacy passed out and not breathing. The sitter was giving her mouth-to-mouth, and the paramedics came in right behind me. They rushed her to the hospital."

"And what was wrong with her?"

"She had been violently shaken, it's what they call shaken baby syndrome. She almost died, but we were lucky."

"Was anyone arrested for this crime?"

"Yes, the sitter was, but she didn't do it."

"Objection!"

"Sustained. Ms. Shaw, I fail to see how this relates to this case in any way. I'm going to have to ask you to move on to another line of questioning and stop wasting the courts time."

"Yes, Your Honor. I'm sorry." But she had gotten the story out about Nathan's little girl. It would come in handy at a later point in time. "So, Melissa, let's get back to your relationship with Nathan Hamilton."

Again, Mr. Benton sprang from his seat. "Objection! Mr. Hamilton is not on trial here."

"Sustained."

Aunt Marty acted as if she had failed, but in reality, she had gotten the jury to hear what they needed to. "No more questions of this witness."

Mr. Benton walked toward the witness box, smirking. "Miss Evans, or is it Mrs.?"

"It's Ms."

"Are you married or not?"

"I'm in the process of getting a divorce."

"So you were married when you were sleeping with both Nathan Hamilton and Collin Chavis?"

"Well, I..."

"Yes or no."

"Yes." She realized he was trying to make her look trashy and unreliable as a witness, but there was nothing she could do.

"So how can you know who the father of your daughter is? It could be just about anyone, now couldn't it?"

"No, Nathan is her father."

"And how could you know that? You were sleeping with at least three men at one time, maybe even more."

"That's not true. I didn't sleep with Collin until after I had the baby."

"But that still leaves your husband, and anyone else that may have come along at that period of time."

"There was no one else but Nathan."

"But isn't it true that you testified at the previous trial that your husband had been the father of your child?"

"Yes. Nathan didn't want anyone to know he was the father."

"So you perjured yourself, is that right, Ms. Evans?"

She looked at Aunt Marty, fear in her eyes. They had discussed that this might happen, but they had hoped Mr. Benton wouldn't recall that statement. "I guess so." Her voice was almost inaudible.

"Excuse me. Could you please speak up, Ms. Evans. Did you perjure yourself at the last trial?"

"Yes."

"Your Honor, I move that all testimony given by this witness be struck from the record. She has proven to be an unreliable witness, admitting to perjury, plus the fact that all her testimony has been totally unrelated."

"I have to agree, Mr. Benton." He glanced at the recorder. "Please strike all of Ms. Evans's testimony from the record. The jury is to forget everything that Ms. Evans has said and not let it sway your verdict in any way."

Mayor Shaw knew that these were just words. Once the jury heard something, they couldn't just forget it. They could try to pretend it won't affect their decision, but every piece of information you can get into their heads will affect how they feel about the case.

The judge addressed Aunt Marty. "Your next witness?"

"I would like to call Sheriff Woolridge."

The sheriff was brought in and placed under oath.

"Sheriff Woolridge, could you please tell us what caused the fire at the Chavis home the night of May 20th of last year?"

"Arson. A clear case of arson."

"What makes you so sure it was arson, and not an accident?"

"There was an obvious odor of an accelerant, a gasoline and fuel oil mixture, in the area of the point of origin."

"Please explain the term 'point of origin' to the jury."

"The point of origin is where the investigators determine the fire began. In this case, it was in the rear of the house, in the kitchen."

"So couldn't it have just been a kitchen fire? Maybe someone left cooking oil on the stove too long?"

"No, Ma'am. There was deep charring and alligatoring that is caused by what's known as flash over. This fire was very intense. This evidence, along with the strong odor of the gasoline and oil, proves that this fire was set on purpose. There is no way a simple kitchen fire would have reached the velocity that this one did so quickly. It was arson."

"So you are telling us that it was definitely arson and that the fire was set in the rear of the house, in the kitchen area. Is this correct?"

"That's right."

"No more questions."

Mr. Benton stood up and held up his hand to the Sheriff. "Before you step down, Sheriff, I would like to ask one or two questions. Did you find the gasoline can that you believe held the fuel that was used to start the fire?"

"Yes, we did find a can that contained a gasoline and oil mixture like the one used as an accelerant in this case."

"And where did you find this can?"

"Behind the steel mill."

"And were there any fingerprints on the can?"

"Yes, Collin Chavis's."

"Thank you."

This evidence was a repeat of his earlier presentation, but he needed to keep the key points clear in the jurors' minds.

Aunt Marty hesitated as she debated over whether to call Raymond to the stand. Most of the information he could contribute had already been established, and what had not been, Rachel could probably convey as well, or maybe better, than Raymond.

"Ms. Shaw? Do you have any other witnesses or not?" The judge was getting impatient.

"Oh, yes, Your Honor."

"In that case, can we get on with it?"

"Of course. My next witness is Rachel Hamilton."

Rachel took a deep breath as she stood. Nathan glared at her as she walked past him and was sworn in.

"For the record, please state your name."

"Rachel Brittain Hamilton."

"Mrs. Hamilton, are you married to Nathan Hamilton?"

"Yes, but not for long. We're in the process of a divorce."

"I see. And why is that?"

"OBJECTION!" Mr. Benton boomed. "This is not the place to air out Mr. and Mrs. Hamilton's dirty laundry."

Aunt Marty raised her hand as if to say "Stop". "You're right, Mr. Benton. I will ask another question."

"Mrs. Hamilton, did you find a diamond ring on a chain as Nathan Hamilton talked about earlier?"

"Yes."

"And just where did you find it?"

"In the ashes in the kitchen area of the house, under a burnt cookie sheet."

"The kitchen was in the rear of the house, is that correct?"

"Yes."

"Who rescued you from the fire?"

"Nathan."

"And did he take you out the back door of the house?"

"No, the front. There was no way anyone could get through the back because of the fire. It had totally engulfed the entire rear of the house."

"Oh, that's right. Mr. Hamilton already testified that he entered the front door and went back out that same way."

"Yes."

"So just how do you think his necklace might have gotten to the rear of the house?" She frowned as if it was a very puzzling situation and zoned out for a few seconds as if in deep thought.

"Objection, grand standing!"

"Over-ruled." The judge was enjoying watching Marty make her case. He could see now where she was headed and was beginning to show more interest. Up to this point, he had looked terribly bored with the entire affair.

"Mrs. Hamilton, was your husband contracted to rebuild the Chavis home?"

"Yes."

"And was he excited about getting this job?"

"Sure. He knew he would get the job since he was such a close friend of the family, and he made comments about what a great opportunity it was for him."

"Oh? What kind of opportunity?"

"Well, he said it would not only bring in plenty of money, but it would elevate his reputation as one of the best home builders around."

"And did it?"

"Oh, yes. He has done extremely well since the fire."

Mr. Benton stood up, thoroughly disgusted. "Objection, Your Honor. Mr. Hamilton is not on trial here. Can we please stick to the facts that are pertinent to this case?"

"Let's move it along, Ms. Shaw," the judge warned.

Nathan had been getting increasingly nervous and decided it was time for him to leave. As he made his way to the aisle, the judge noticed him.

"Mr. Hamilton. I suggest you do not leave the courthouse. Ms. Shaw has asked that she be allowed to recall you as a witness. So you must remain available."

Nathan nodded in agreement and exited the courtroom.

Aunt Marty scratched her head and faced the jury, talking to herself. "Now I wonder why he would want to leave?"

The judge shook his head and gave her a look of caution. "Ms. Shaw, please proceed with your witness."

After considering for a moment whether to ask any more questions, she shook her head. "No more questions."

Mr. Benton rose confidently. "Mrs. Hamilton. You seem to be trying to convince this court that your husband committed this crime, and not the defendant. Is there a reason for that?"

"If that's the way it looks to you, Mr. Benton, it's because that's the way the facts add up."

"Didn't you tell us that you are divorcing Mr. Hamilton?"

"Yes."

"During divorce, there can be a lot of animosity, maybe even extreme hatred. Isn't that so?"

"And what are you saying?" She knew what he was trying to make her say, but she just looked confused and innocent.

"I'm saying that you are angry with your husband and are trying to railroad him."

It was Marty's turn to object. "Argumentative."

"Sustained."

Mr. Benton ignored them as he stared into Rachel's eyes, trying to intimidate her. "Mrs. Hamilton, what is your relationship with the defendant?"

She glanced at Collin. "He's my father's son."

"Oh, no he isn't. He is the son of your father's wife, but he is no blood relation to you."

"Well, that's true, but he thinks of himself still as Raymond Chavis's son."

"But how do you feel about him?"

"I care about him."

"A great deal, don't you? Would you say that you love him?"

"Yes. At one time I thought he was my brother. Of course, I love him."

"No, no, no. Mrs. Hamilton." He shook his head, looked at the jury and raised his voice. "Are you in love with Collin Chavis?"

The courtroom was so hushed Rachel could hear the clock on the back wall ticking. Her eyes met Collin's as she tried to figure out what to say. But Aunt Marty came to the rescue. "Objection. What Rachel feels for Collin Chavis has no bearing on this case whatsoever."

"Oh, contraire, Ms. Shaw. If she is in love with the defendant, then she might be willing to slant the truth so she can save his hide."

It didn't matter what her answer was to the question now, the damage had been done. The jury had already been swayed to some degree by the suggestion.

The judge reminded the attorneys to address their comments to the court and not to each other. Then he asked Mr. Benton to proceed.

Satisfied that he'd made his point and neutralized her testimony, he gave her an arrogant smirk. "No more questions for this witness." The way he'd said 'this witness' indicated that she was too worthless to continue questioning.

Rachel started to stand when Aunt Marty spoke up. "One minute, Rachel. Your Honor, I would like to ask a couple more questions."

"Go ahead." He was sounding bored again, or maybe just tired.

"Mrs. Hamilton. Have you ever had sexual relations with Collin Chavis?" She knew this could be a dangerous question since she wasn't completely sure of the answer, but she had to take the chance.

"No, of course not."

"Have you ever been unfaithful in your marriage?"

"No."

"Do you hate your husband?"

"No." *I don't hate him; I just hate what he did.* She tried to convince herself she was telling the truth. She saw Nathan standing in the rear of the courtroom and wondered when he had slipped back in.

"Why are you divorcing him?"

Mr. Benton jumped to his feet. She was undoing everything he had done! "Objection!"

The judge peeked up at him. "You're the one that opened this can of worms, Mr. Benton. Answer the question, Mrs. Hamilton."

"I am divorcing him because he has destroyed my love for him."

"And how did he do that?"

"Among other things, by drinking too much, abusing his daughter, and killing Lucille Chavis." She looked straight at him as the courtroom erupted into mass confusion. The media cameras were going crazy, and the prosecuting attorney was screaming. "OBJECTION!!"

The judge's gavel crashed down on the desk several times before he could gain control of the courtroom. "Order! I will have order in my court right now or I will clear the courtroom!" Everyone began to calm down as he hammered the gavel one more time. "Mr. Benton, your objection is sustained. Ms. Shaw, are you finished with this witness?"

"Yes, Your Honor."

"Mrs. Hamilton, you may step down." He looked at his watch. It was approaching 4:30 and had been a long day. "Ms. Shaw, how many more witnesses do you have?"

"One, possibly two."

"Do you want to proceed now or continue tomorrow morning?"

Aunt Marty was worried that Nathan might skip town if he got away from the courthouse today. "I believe we can finish this up today. I don't foresee this taking much longer."

"Very well, proceed."

"I'd like to call Frank Jennings to the stand."

Mr. Jennings was sworn in, and Aunt Marty smiled warmly at him as she approached him. "Please tell the court your full name and occupation."

"Franklin Roosevelt Jennings. I'm one of the owners of H & J Construction Company."

"H & J standing for Hamilton and Jennings, correct?"

"Yes, I'm partners with Nathan Hamilton."

"Now, Mr. Jennings, tell us about how you learned of your company obtaining the contract to rebuild the Chavis residence after the fire."

"Well, I was in the office working on a bid for a small room addition when Nathan came busting through the door all excited. He started going on about how we could relax about the money situation because our ship had come in."

"Had the business been struggling?"

"Yes, the cash flow wasn't doing real good at that time. We were just getting enough small jobs to barely keep afloat."

"And when was this that Mr. Hamilton came in with this news, what date?"

"Oh it was the day after the Chavis' house had burned down. I remember because I had just read about it in the paper that morning. There were pictures on the front page of the blazing structure."

"So how would Nathan know your company would get the job to rebuild, or was that what he was talking about when he said your ship had come in?"

"Oh, yeah, that's what he went on and on about. And I asked him that very question, how did he know we would get the job."

"And what was his answer?"

"Just for me not to worry about it. He said he was working on it, and he had everything under control. I didn't know what he meant, and just sort of shrugged it off and went back to work."

"So what happened after that?"

"Oh he just kept talking about how he was gonna get us this job and how it would put our company on top. Then he said he had this plan to finally get what was rightfully his and put things the way they were suppose to be."

"What on earth could he have meant by that?"

"I had no idea then, but I've heard him bragging since then about how he had taken Collin's woman and his birthright. He really hated Collin, that was obvious. But I never figured out why."

Mr. Benton rose to his feet. "Your Honor, once again, Mr. Hamilton is not on trial here. Could we please get the focus back on the defendant."

The judge gave him a crooked smile. "Yes, Mr. Benton, I'm sure that is what you would prefer. Ms. Shaw, does this witness have any knowledge about the night of the fire or other pertinent facts on this case?"

"Judge, this witness has given us evidence that someone other than the defendant had motive to set that fire. I only have one more question for him."

"Proceed."

"Mr. Jennings, your company did end up rebuilding the Chavis home, and that job DID make your company very successful, is that right?"

"Oh, yes Ma'am. No doubt about that!"

"Thank you."

Mr. Benton stood but did not bother to approach. "Mr. Jennings, isn't it possible that Mr. Hamilton was just so sure of getting the job to rebuild the Chavis house simply because he was a close friend of their family and that he was excited about rebuilding simply because it is a beautiful home that ANY builder would enjoy building?"

"Well, yeah, but...."

"And isn't it possible that his anger toward Collin Chavis was because he believed him guilty of this horrendous crime?"

"I believe it was more than that, 'cause he always disliked Collin."

"Dislike is a far cry from hate, Mr. Jennings. No more questions."

Aunt Marty thought about her brother, Tom. He was Raymond's partner at the steel mill and Collin's boss at the time of the fire. He could be a good character witness, but he'd requested that she not call on him. His heart wasn't strong, and he was an extremely nervous person, so she'd decided to call him only if absolutely necessary. She glanced over her notes and felt that the case was going well enough that she didn't need him.

"Judge, I would ask that the defendant, Collin Chavis be called next."

Collin sat in the witness chair facing the courtroom. Rachel's heart-rate increased, and she became just as nervous as when she had been sitting up there. *He is so sexy!* She closed her eyes and scolded. *This is not the time to be thinking about that!* However, when she opened her eyes and saw him looking at her, a warm current surged through her causing a vaginal contraction as uncontrollable as a hiccup.

"Collin, please tell us, in your own words, what happened the night of the fire."

"Nathan had taken Rachel out to dinner. I was feeling a little jealous and, after he dropped her off and went home, I went to his house to tell him to stay away from her."

"Had you been drinking?"

"No."

"So what happened when you got there?"

"Nathan listened to what I had to say about him leaving Rachel alone, and then he invited me in so we could talk about the situation. He offered me a drink, and I accepted. We sat down, and he was really understanding about my feelings toward Rachel. I thought we had come to an understanding and he was going to respect my wishes. We had a couple more drinks, and the next thing I remember is waking up in my car behind the steel mill."

"And how did you feel when you woke up?"

"Groggy, like I'd been drugged."

"Or like you were drunk?"

"No, I've been drunk before but this was different. I don't know how to describe it."

"So then what did you do?"

"I tried to remember how I'd gotten to the steel mill, but I couldn't remember leaving Nathan's house at all. I just began driving, no destination in mind, and wound up in Turtle Creek."

"Do you work at the steel mill?"

"Yes."

"And what do you do there?"

"I supervise the machinists."

"So do you just walk around and watch them, or do you have other duties?"

The prosecutor sat slumped in his chair and rolled his eyes. "Objection, Your Honor. Relevance?" He tried to sound bored, hoping the judge would feel the same.

Aunt Marty looked at the judge and smiled politely, "I'm getting there, I promise."

"Proceed."

"Do you remember the question, Collin?"

"Yes, I do have other duties. I have to be sure the equipment is maintained properly and that all safety rules are followed."

"If a machine goes down, who fixes it?"

"Well, we have maintenance personnel, but if it's a simple matter of gassing it up, I sometimes do that rather than bother the maintenance crew."

"So you would handle gas cans on occasion?"

"Sure, all the time."

"And do these machines run on just pure gasoline?"

"No, most of them use a gasoline and oil mixture." He finally had figured out where his aunt was going with her line of questioning, and so had everyone else.

"I see. So the gasoline can behind the steel mill that contained a gasoline and oil mixture AND had your fingerprints on it was really not such a mystery, was it?"

"Not at all."

"No more questions"

Mr. Benton stood but again did not bother to leave his table. "Mr. Chavis, how do you know you did not commit this crime if you don't remember leaving Mr. Hamilton's house and don't know how you got to the steel mill?"

"All I know is that I wouldn't have done such a thing. I loved everyone in that house and would never have done anything to hurt any of them."

"But you have already admitted to being upset. People do things when they are upset that they might not normally do, isn't that true?"

"Not to this extreme. I didn't do it, I'm sure of that."

Unable to get Collin rattled, Mr. Benton decided to quit before he only made things worse. "No more questions."

Aunt Marty stood and smiled at the judge. "One last witness, Your Honor, and I'll make it quick."

"Okay, then we'll have closing arguments in the morning. Call your witness."

"I call Nathaniel Hamilton back to the stand."

Nathan looked defeated as he began making his way back to the front of the courtroom. Then he took a deep breath and tried to look confident as he reached the witness box and was reminded that he was still under oath.

Aunt Marty looked at Nathan with kind eyes, then frowned as if she were very confused. "Nathan, I need you to clear up some facts for me if you will. First of all, how do you explain the conflicting stories about Collin's visit to your house that night? You say he arrived drunk, and you offered him coffee. He says he arrived sober, and you offered him several drinks. Which was it?"

"He's telling a lie trying to save his own skin. Isn't that obvious?"

"But if you invited him in and offered him coffee to help sober him up and talked to him for a while, how do you explain that he can't remember anything about leaving your home?"

"Again, he's lying."

"Well, someone is, that's for sure."

Mr. Benton was too tired to object. He just wanted this day to be over.

"Okay, so let's move on to something else I don't understand. How do you explain that the jewelry that belonged to you, that you say you lost the night of the fire, was found by Rachel in the KITCHEN area of the house?"

"I told you I lost it when I ran in to rescue Rachel."

"Yes, but you also said you came in the front door and back out the front door. You never went into the back part of the house. And, according to previous testimony, no one could have been in that part of the house because the fire had totally engulfed that area by the time you arrived to perform this rescue. So how did this ring get in the KITCHEN area of the house?"

He squirmed in his seat. "I don't know. Maybe it got kicked around after the fire."

She smiled and placed her forefinger to her chin. "You know, I thought of that. But Rachel said she had to kick a cookie sheet out of the way before she noticed the ring hidden in a pile of ashes. Somehow, I find it hard to believe it just got kicked under there."

"Well, I don't know how else it got there."

"Oh I think you do, but let's continue, shall we?"

"Please do," Mr. Benton muttered, and the judge nodded agreement.

"Okay, Mr. Hamilton. How did you feel about you and your father struggling to build a company, and Mr. and Mrs. Chavis were living a life of luxury? Did that bother you at all?"

"Sometimes."

"I bet you felt like Justin and Collin were better than you because they were well off, right?"

"No. I never felt like that. They may have had money, but they still had their family skeletons. They were no better than anyone else."

"So you were never jealous of Justin or Collin. Is that what you're saying?"

He smirked, "I certainly had no reason to be jealous of Collin."

"How did you feel about Lucille Chavis?"

"She was okay. I didn't feel much of anything towards her."

"Come on now, Nathan. You expect for us to believe that this woman had an affair with your father and destroyed your family, and you didn't feel any animosity toward her at all?"

"Maybe when I was a kid. But I got over it."

"I doubt that. That is not something one gets over that easily."

He looked down at his lap so no one could read his face. He wasn't quite sure what he should do or say, so he just sat there, waiting.

"I bet you were pretty excited when Mr. Chavis chose you to rebuild his home, weren't you?"

"Sure. I was pretty sure he would let me do it since I've been like part of the family for years."

"And building a home like that certainly did a lot for your company prestige, wouldn't you say?"

"Well, yeah. It's a beautiful home and rebuilding it was a great accomplishment. I'm pretty proud of how it turned out, too."

"But if it had never burned down, you would never have had that opportunity. Isn't that ironic how the Chavis's misfortune did so much for you."

He looked as if he had been slapped and suddenly snapped to attention. "That's the way life is sometimes. There are even some businesses that feed on other people's misfortunes. Not that that's what I did. It just worked out that way."

"Of course it did." It was obvious by her sarcastic tone that she didn't believe a word he was saying. "And then there was Rachel."

"What about her?" He was on the defensive now. He wasn't just answering questions anymore.

Aunt Marty smiled, not to be friendly, but because she had him scared. "Well, you were in love with her and rescuing her from the fire made you her hero. Right?"

"Maybe. I'm just glad I was there."

"Another fine coincidence. And with Collin in prison for the arson charge, you had a wide open field to pursue her, didn't you?"

"It's not my fault he went to jail. He deserved what he got."

"Maybe. But isn't it wonderful how all these horrible things seemed to just help you in every way. First you were able to get rid of Lucille Chavis, the woman that had destroyed your family. You were able to get rid of Collin Chavis, the man that stood in your way of winning the woman you wanted. And you were able to obtain a building contract that was a dream of a lifetime for most contractors. The Chavises lost everything, but you managed to gain everything. How ironic is that?"

He couldn't hide the gleam in his eye as he glanced at Collin. But he tried desperately to look as if nothing she had said touched him at all. "That's just the way things happen sometimes."

"No more questions, Your Honor." She gave Nathan an evil look and shook her head in disgust.

"Mr. Benton." Judge Carlisle just wanted to go home. It was past dinnertime, and his stomach was beginning to burn with hunger.

The prosecuting attorney stood as if he were ready to cross-examine, then changed his mind. "No questions."

The judge's relief showed on his face. "Thank you. Court is dismissed and will reconvene tomorrow morning at 9:00."

Rachel remained in the courtroom waiting for the commotion to die down in the hallway. The media frenzy could be heard through the closed double doors, and she didn't feel up to fighting her way through the mob. She crept back to the back corner of the room so if anyone glanced in they might miss seeing her. Taking a deep breath, she began to contemplate all that had happened in the past year. She had barely been able to process it all. Eastridge had become her home. Her entire life was here. The house in Wapiti had been sold to Mr. Jamison, and the money she had received from the sale was in the bank just waiting for her to get on with her life. But she couldn't even think of that until Collin was free and Nathan was behind bars where he belonged. *Hopefully after tomorrow we can all get on with our lives.*

The noise seemed to be subsiding, so she walked to the doors and peeked out. The hallway was clear of the cameras and reporters, and it sounded as if they were outside moving away from the building. She slipped into the hall and walked to the exit. She stood there, peeking out of the window now and then, being careful not to be seen, waiting for all the cameras and microphones to be packed up. There were a couple of reporters looming near her car, obviously waiting for her to emerge. *My car.* She thought lovingly of her little red car and of Raymond and Lucille. When she had received the money from the sale of her mountain home, she had offered to pay for the car. But Raymond had insisted that Lucille would have wanted her to have it. So he had put the title in her name and given it to her as soon as Lucille's estate had been settled.

She glanced out of the window again just in time to see one of the reporters returning to the building, probably in search of her. She thought about retreating to the restroom, but decided not to. She braced herself, confidently shoved the door open and began a fast and determined beeline to her vehicle. As the reporter raised her microphone, Rachel held her hand up and, looking the woman in the eye with a deadly stare, shook her head. Although there had been no words spoken, the inexperienced young reporter got the message loud and clear to leave her alone and backed away. Rachel had been lucky that the young lady had not yet acquired the blood-thirsty aggressiveness of the more accomplished hounds.

CHAPTER 20

One year later

After his father died, Nathan had become consumed with bitterness. He vowed to get even with Lucille for ruining his family. For years he'd watched Collin, his half brother, live an extravagant lifestyle that he himself could only sample when he visited their home under the pretense of being a friend. Then lovely Rachel had shown up giving Nathan the perfect opportunity to take from Collin the one thing he knew he wanted more than anything money could buy. He'd bided his time, carefully waiting for the perfect occasion. That night when Collin had shown up at his door, Nathan quickly decided to take advantage of his vulnerable mood. He'd offered him several drinks, slipping sleeping pills into the mixture. After Collin had passed out on the sofa, Nathan slipped outside, placed his bike into the back of his truck, and drove to the steel mill, parking a block down the road. Then he'd pedaled back to his house, put on some gloves, removed Collin's keys from his pocket, and loaded Collin into the passenger seat of his little sports car. He then drove Collin's car to the steel mill and grabbed the gasoline can, drove to the Chavis home and entered through the unlocked rear door, poured the gasoline over the kitchen floor and ignited it with a match, then quickly sped off back to the steel mill. This way the only tracks that would be noticed by the police around the Chavis home would be from Collin's car. When he arrived back at the steel mill, he placed Collin into the driver's seat and placed the gas can where it would be easily found by the police. Then he ran to his truck and raced to the Chavis house to rescue Rachel.

The plan had been so perfect. He still didn't understand how Marty had figured it all out, but here he sat in a jail cell awaiting his appeal. His attorney had assured him that he would get off. Although he'd had motive and opportunity, the only hard evidence they had against him was that damn ring on the chain that had been found in the kitchen area of the house.

And even if he did get off for the arson and murder, he still had to do time for the child abuse charge. There was no getting out of that one. Rachel had really screwed him with that tape where he'd confessed. But he'd only received eighteen months. That shouldn't be too difficult.

Suddenly the guard unlocked his cell. "You've got a visitor." He led him through the halls to the visitation room and sat him down at the metal table.

I wonder who could be visiting me. I certainly don't have any friends left in this town. It must be my lawyer.

He watched as a small fragile-looking woman in her mid to late forties entered the room. She had bottled blond hair and looked familiar—"Mother?"

"You remember me?" She looked unsure of approaching her son.

"I had pictures." He could barely speak. He felt numb, as if he were in a strange dream. "I thought you were dead—. Since I hadn't heard from you."

"I'm sorry about that." She walked slowly to the table and sat down, her eyes never leaving his. "I wanted to contact you, but was afraid of disrupting your life. But then I read about your troubles here and had to see if I could help you in any way."

He smirked at her and shook his head. "I think you're a little late for that. I could have used your help for the past twenty years, but you weren't around. So why now?"

"You're right." She looked down and stood, holding to the table to steady herself. "Maybe this was a mistake. I shouldn't have come." She started toward the door.

His voice thundered through the room. "Don't you dare leave!" Suddenly he was that five year old again, and the tears began to flow. "Please don't leave again."

She turned to look at him, tears dripping down her cheeks. "I'm sorry I left you, but I'm here now." She walked toward him to put her arms around him, but was stopped by the guard.

Rachel sat beside her mother's grave silently watching the goldenrod and anemone sway in the blustery summer breeze that was blowing across a nearby meadow. A warm gust reached the cemetery and kissed her face. She smiled. "Momma, Mr. Jamison has taken good care of our old home. He's planted flowers and kept the yard nice."

She sat contemplating all that had happened to her since she'd left Wapiti. "It's been quite an adventure for me since you left me. So much has happened to get me to where I am today." She placed her hand over her stomach as she felt a slight flutter. A shadow fell over her, and she looked up to see Collin standing nearby. She giggled with excitement. "Come here!"

"What is it?"

"I just felt our baby move for the first time!"

He knelt beside her and took her in his arms. "I've got to be the luckiest man in the world." He helped her to her feet, placed his arm around her shoulder, and they began to walk slowly back across the cemetery. There in the front yard of her old home place was Aunt Marty and Mr. Jamison, laughing and talking like old friends.

Rachel raised an eyebrow. "Well, looks like those two are getting along rather well, wouldn't you say?"

"Yeah, I don't think I've ever seen Aunt Marty quite so giddy."

"I know. I really hate to tear her away to go back home, but Dad should be getting home soon, and I want to be there."

"Me too. I hope he had a good visit with Justin, Trisha and little Lucy."

"I'm sure he did. Justin said Dad was having trouble keeping up with Lucy. She's pretty fast on those pudgy little legs for a child that's not even two yet. I wish we could visit them. I'd love to see her."

"Well, I talked to Justin yesterday, and he said they'd come for a visit before the summer is over."

"Really?! That's great! Maybe I'll be able to get some time off so I can spend lots of time with them."

"Well, I guess it won't be long before you'll have to take time off. You won't be able to fit in those slinky fashions much longer. You're beginning to bulge already."

"No problem. I'll just model the maternity fashions that I'm designing." She peeked up at him and grinned.

"You're designing? When did you start doing that?"

She laughed as they walked across the road and joined Mr. Jamison and Aunt Marty. "I'll tell you all about it later. Just suffice it to say that I've been promoted."

Rachel watched the cliffs and trees go by as they wound their way back down the mountain towards home. Aunt Marty sat in the back seat of Collin's SUV talking incessantly about what a nice man Nick Jamison is. Collin reached over and took Rachel's hand and smiled, keeping his eyes on the winding road. She closed her eyes, and a wave of serenity caressed her. She had it all; a wonderful husband, a great family, a beautiful baby on the way, an expanding career that she loved, and a beautiful home. The white plantation-style house of which she had been in such awe when she had seen it for the first time, was now her home. The love between herself, Collin, and her father filled the home so completely that the fire and rebuilding just seemed like a horrible nightmare. *Life is good!* Collin squeezed her hand as Aunt Marty's rambling stopped, and her snoring took its place.

Printed in the United States
19651LVS00003B/160-204